THE SHADOWS OF THE BIG EAST
A DETECTIVE MYSTERY AND CRIME THRILLER

FROM THE CINEMATIC WORLD
OF DING DONG DITCH

BY NOZ

BROUGHT TO YOU BY THE CINEMATIC WORLD OF DING DONG DITCH™
Scan Here
To Watch Movie
DING DONG
DITCH
THE SHADOWS OF THE BIG EAST
SCENE DO NOT C
WRITTEN BY NOZ
A NOZ CRIME THRILLER
BOOK AND MOVIE OUT NOW
A DETECTIVE MYSTERY AND CRIME THRILLER
MAXVISIONFILMS.COM
3

A MESSAGE FROM THE AUTHORS

Every moment, countless individuals fall victim to human trafficking and displacement. We stand firm in our commitment to raise awareness, provide relief, and support organizations fighting for those in need.

We at MaxVision will continue to build water wells, safe havens for women, and shelters for children to ensure they have protection, security, and a future.

We are all one. God bless the planet.

-Team Mavision

Decide what comes next.

www.Maxvisionfilms.com

Now, back to your regularly scheduled programming:

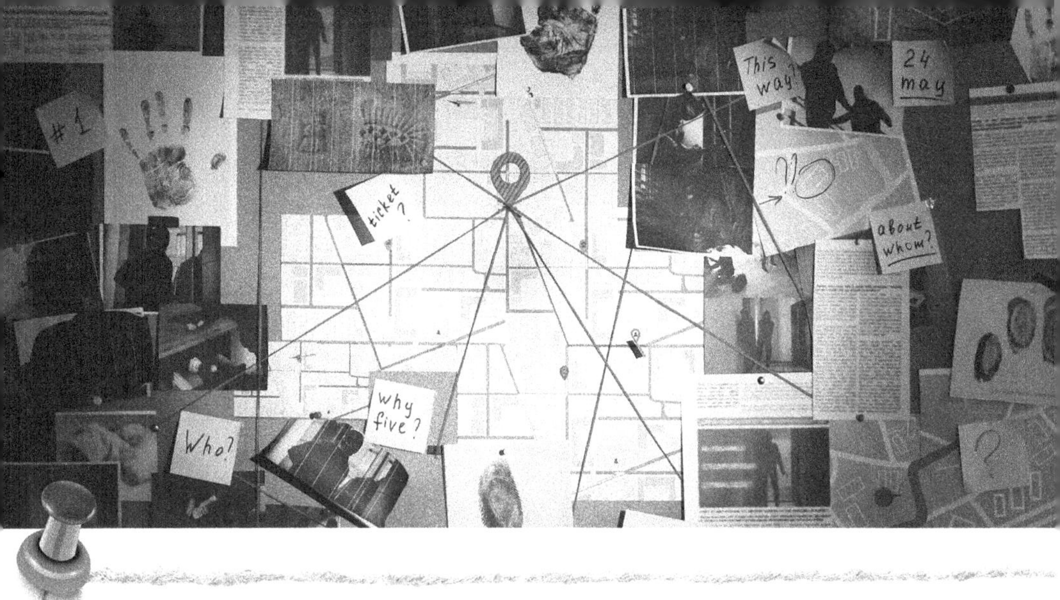

Ding Dong Ditch™ book and movie is a high-octane, action-packed thriller that burrows deep into the murkiness of power, corruption, and loyalty. With every unraveled clue, the stakes increase, the enemies become more ruthless, and the consequences become even deadlier. As Dawson and his rookie team of detectives get closer to the truth, they discover secrets that will destroy them and the city.

With a heart-pounding pace and a killer ending, **Ding Dong Ditch**™ leaves readers questioning just how far justice can go and what it truly costs. It's a suspenseful mystery thriller that keeps audiences guessing until the very last page.

In a city where every clue is a trap, and every answer leads to another lie, how far will one detective go to uncover the truth?

DOCKET FILES

PROLOGUE

A KNOCK AT THE WRONG DOOR

OCTOBER 30TH – 8:42 PM

Some kids spent Mischief Night at home; watching horror movies and indulging in candy. Not Lucas, Oliver, and Jake. For them, this night was tradition, a rite of passage.

Lucas, a consummate planner—sharp, quick-witted, and just reckless enough to keep things interesting—always wrote the blueprint for their misadventures. Oliver, his right-hand man, brought the muscle and the nerve, ready to back whatever wild idea Lucas cooked up. And then there was Jake: the wildcard. The smooth talker. He could charm his way out of anything. Or at least, he thought he could.

The plan was simple: gather supplies, map out their targets, and make sure by morning, everyone was talking—but no one had a clue who to blame.

There was a feeling in the air the boys couldn't shake—unspoken, but heavy. This year was different.

Coins clattered onto the wooden floor of the clubhouse. Lucas and Oliver knelt beside an overturned piggy bank, sifting through quarters, dimes, and pennies. The loose change glittered beneath the battery-powered lantern hanging from the ceiling as their fingers worked fast to count the pile.

Lucas grinned, tossing a crumpled bill on top. "Nineteen dollars and twenty-two cents."

Oliver snorted. "Damn, that's it? We barely got enough."

Lucas shrugged. "Enough for what we need."

Jake stepped inside, still wearing the hoodie he'd worn to school, grinning like he owned the world. "What's good, fellas?"

Lucas and Oliver dumped the coins into a backpack. "We got nineteen twenty-two," said Lucas. "Enough for TP, paper bags, and maybe a lighter."

Jake nodded. "Alright, let's roll."

Lucas slung the backpack over his shoulder, and the three grabbed their bikes, kicking off into the cool October night.

Not far off, inside a time-weathered house that rested atop a slight hill, the muffled blare of heavy metal music cut through the stillness of a dimly lit street. With the thudding of the bassline, flakes of old paint rattled loose from the peeling shutters and drifted onto the parched grass.

In the living room, a vintage boombox sat on a battered coffee table, its surface scarred with cigarette burns and coffee ring stains.

Tom Caldwell slouched on a threadbare couch, his muscular frame wrapped in worn fatigues and a torn tank top. He hunched his broad shoulders, dark eyes fixed on the collection of photographs and medals strewn across the table.

The room functioned almost as a museum: a shrine to the man he used to be. War medals gleamed under the flickering light of a single lamp, their polished surfaces at odds with the room's quiet decay. Tom picked up a group photo, his rough fingers tracing the faces frozen in time. A faint smile ghosted his lips.

"I miss you guys," he murmured, his voice gravelly from disuse and whiskey. "Those were the days…"

His smile faded as his gaze shifted to another photo, a snapshot of a boy with a beaming smile and bright eyes. Sandy blond hair, just like his used to be, before the gray began its advance. His son.

"Tommy," Tom whispered, voice cracking. The name hung in the air, fragile, a ghost of a life that had been ripped away. "I should've been there." His grip tightened around the photo. "What kind of father am I?"

The question lingered, unanswered, as the memory of his ex-wife intruded. Samantha's face flickered on the muted television in the corner, her warm smile on the lifted footage nothing but a bitter reminder. The image of her holding hands with her soon to be husband sent a fresh wave of anger surging through him.

"Till death do us part," Tom hissed, low and venomous. "Guess that didn't include our son's death, huh?" The whiskey bottle wobbled as his fist slammed down on the table. "You fucking traitor!" he bellowed.

The heavy metal music swelled, drowning out his own voice. The dilapidated house seemed to tremble under the weight of his rage.

Tom leaned back to stare at the ceiling, the fight draining from his body. The music roared on, offering no solace, no escape. His chest heaved with ragged breaths, each one throbbing with regret.

Outside, the city pulsed with life—kids darting between houses, their laughter sharp and fleeting, sneakers slapping against the pavement as they vanished into the night. Doors slammed. Shouts rang out. The thrill of the chase, the game, the ritual. It was Mischief Night, and the streets belonged to the reckless.

But inside that dimly lit house, just beyond the cracked blinds, Tom only sat, shoulders hunched, a silhouette swallowed by the clutter of a life gone wrong. To him, the walls felt tighter every night, inching closer, whispering things he didn't want to hear. It was no longer air he breathed, but stale smoke, his own sweat, and the lingering ghost of something burnt. His fingers twitched against his knee, restless.

Tom sat in silence. The door bells had rung all night—but he never moved. Just sat there, still as stone.

Kids came and went. Some didn't make it up the hill. But one did.

One single ring.

A brave soul made it to the top. Pressed it.

Ding.

Tom didn't flinch. Not yet.

He stared at the clock. Something about the time…

Something pulled at him.

Without thinking, he ominously reached for his pager—Pressed a button he never touched.

Then he stood up.

9:06 PM

The night stretched ahead, full of promise. Oliver, Lucas, and Jake glided through the backstreets, dark hoodies blending with the shadows. Their footsteps were light, hands in pockets, always moving, never pausing.

The familiar glow of the corner store loomed ahead, an island of neon humming against the cold air. Checkpoint. Supplier. One last stop before the night truly began. The bell over the door jangled as they stepped inside.

Dust had settled on the shelves, ripe with the musty smell of old spices. The floorboards creaked underfoot. Behind the worn counter, the old clerk scarcely stirred, observing the three boys. His eyes were sharp, sunken deep into a weathered face that had seen more than its share of long nights. He didn't speak—just tracked them; slow and steady.

Lucas slipped down an aisle, trailing his fingers over cans of soup, pretending to browse. Jake drifted toward the counter, hands plunged deep in the front of his hoodie. Oliver nudged Lucas, a silent signal: *Stick to the plan.* They needed paper bags for the dog poop, toilet paper for the trees, eggs for everything, and a lighter for the finishing touch.

Jake leaned on the counter, flashing his best *I'm-just-a-stupid-kid* grin. "Hell of a night, huh?" he said.

The clerk didn't answer. Didn't move. Just regarded the three of them.

Oliver grabbed a roll of toilet paper, tossing it in the air once before catching it. Lucas stacked a few items on the counter, calculating a quick distraction.

The old man's fingers twitched.

Jake saw it. Felt it.

Shit.

He shifted, playing it off. "Need a lighter, too."

"No lighters," the man replied.

Jake's grin didn't drop, but it froze just a little.

"No lighters?" Oliver repeated, pulling out a couple of crumpled bills.

The clerk's gaze flickered to the register, then back to the boys.

Jake exhaled, stepping back. "The mission is over," he whispered. They gathered their bags, moving slow and deliberate.

Outside, the street was quieter now; the store's neon signage hummed behind them. The boys shivered, still feeling that watchful gaze, even through the glass.

Lucas kicked a loose rock on the sidewalk. "Well, that sucked."

Oliver sighed.

Jake, however, grinned and produced from his pocket a thin metal lighter. He flicked it open with a soft snick, and the tiny flame flickered, illuminating his smirk.

"Guess again."

Oliver and Lucas stared. "*No way…*"

Their grins stretched wide: The mission was back on. They jumped onto their bikes, wheels kicking up leaves, the night thrumming with potential.

10:32 PM

As always, they started small.

A bag of dog shit, lit and dropped on a porch; an old man cursed as he stepped right into it, his shouts carrying down the block. Eggs cracked against car windows. Toilet paper spiraled through the air, wrapping tree branches like ghostly streamers.

It was exhilarating.

It was *daring*.

Each prank pushed them further, the rush amplifying the thrill that only came from knowing they shouldn't be doing this.

At one point, they spotted a cop car creeping down the street.

They didn't even think—just darted behind trees, pressing their backs against the scaly bark, holding their breath.

The car rolled past.

"That was way too close," Oliver muttered.

Lucas said nothing. Suddenly, there was unease gnawing at his gut, unshakable. His bright blue eyes scanned the surroundings, his mind alive with excitement. Yet something was off. Something about this night, this street, felt different.

"This is it." Oliver's eyes widened as he stared up at the ominous-looking structure perched on a slight hill. It seemed separate from the other houses—still part of the city, yet isolated by a strange darkness. He vibrated with anticipation; completing this challenge would earn them bragging rights for years to come.

Jake, always the instigator, wore a wicked grin. "This guy'll deserve it. He's a total grouch."

Oliver sniffed. "I heard his son died in the war."

Jake balked, "Whatever, man."

Rolls of toilet paper in hand, the boys stepped onto the curb at the end of the long driveway. Lucas suppressed a chill.

"Alright, Lucas, your turn." Jake's voice broke through his thoughts, low with mischief. "I dare you."

"Why me?" Lucas shot back, surprised at the tremor in his own voice.

Oliver balked, "Because you're the fastest, duh." Quickly, he added, "And I already rang the last two."

Lucas rolled his eyes. "Yeah, but this one has a long-ass driveway. And it's on a hill…"

Oliver sighed. "Tell you what. I'll do your homework for a week."

Lucas snorted. "From the guy who got a forty-two on his last test?"

"Okay, fine. I'll get my older sister to do it."

Lucas raised an eyebrow. "Tempting…"

"Plus, no one ever answers the door here," Jake added. "Don't be a wimp!"

Lucas glanced sideways up at the house—the one that was always dark, always still, the house nobody ever visited. The flickering porch light cast a sickly yellow glow over its weathered exterior. As he climbed, the air seemed to grow colder, almost like the house

itself repelled life from it. His heart raced, and a knot formed in his stomach. But to back out now would only invite the ridicule of his two friends.

"Hey, Lucas! Watch this…" Oliver whispered suddenly. He pulled out a carton of eggs, grinning wide, his eyes gleaming with youthful rebellion. Clearly, the adrenaline from their earlier pranks still coursed through him, and he was eager for one more thrill before the night ended.

Lucas hesitated. "Are you sure about this?" he asked, his voice barely a whisper. He glanced back towards the street, half-expecting a busybody neighbor to catch them in the act.

"Come on, don't be a chicken." Oliver moved lightly on his feet, tossing the first egg at the front door. The egg splattered on the wood with a sharp crack that echoed down the otherwise still street, like the clang of a warning bell.

The three burst into giggles. To Lucas, though, his own laugh sounded hollow, his conscience already on him.

Jake checked his phone and smirked. "Man, I gotta bounce. My girl's calling."

"Come on." Oliver scoffed. He looked down at the time blazing across the screen—11:42. "Well, leave us your phone, at least."

Jake clutched it tighter. "No way. I gotta secure these buns."

Lucas shook his head while Oliver groaned. "Fine. We'll finish up."

Jake waved them off, disappearing into the dark. In truth, Lucas wanted to stop, too. He felt in his gut that they'd already pushed their luck too far. But Oliver nudged him. "Come on, man. We've still got supplies."

Reluctantly, Lucas followed him up the rest of the driveway. The house sat in eerie silence, shrouded in something neither of them had noticed before: a camouflaged military net draped over parts of the exterior, blending into the darkness.

Oliver grinned, holding up the last two bags. "Alright, we hit this one, and we're legends."

Lucas swallowed hard and bent down onto the asphalt. His lighter refused to catch. He flicked it again. "Damn thing won't stay lit," he muttered, shaking it.

Oliver took a step back. "Just hurry up, man."

Lucas surveyed the porch. It had two distinct landings: The first was solid concrete, contrasting with the second, which was wooden, with creaky steps leading to the door. With each step he took, dread pressed further down on him.

To his surprise, Oliver began to ease back.

"Come on, man, help me light this," Lucas said.

Oliver nodded, but didn't move forward. Lucas sighed and pressed on, crouching near the doorstep. Finally, the lighter flickered to life, its flame momentarily illuminating the bag before he set it down. He rang the doorbell.

"I did it!" he whispered triumphantly, turning to run.

Then, the darkness moved.

A massive figure lunged from the shadows, grabbing Lucas in a blur, his body twisting mid-air. The breath was knocked from his lungs as he was yanked inside the house, and the door slammed shut behind him.

Oliver's heart nearly stopped. He took a step back, then another.

THUMP.

A sound from beneath the porch. Oliver's eyes darted downward—a rope, coiled and waiting like a snake. Instinct kicked in, and he lifted his right leg to step over it—

Too late.

The rope snapped tight around his left leg, yanking him off balance. Before he could react, his skull slammed against the concrete.

Stars exploded in his vision. His ears rang. Pain flooded his senses.

But it wasn't over.

A mechanical whir churned from beneath the porch, hidden pulleys and tension systems clicking into motion. The rope constricted, pulling Oliver downward, dragging his stunned, disoriented body toward the open space beneath the steps. His head smacked against the wood, his shoulders scraping as he was wrenched through the narrow opening.

The lid snapped shut behind him with eerie finality as he was dragged into the belly of the house.

12:01 AM

Across town, in the bustling precinct of Big East Police Headquarters, the air was thick with doubt and murmurs. Fluorescent lights buzzed overhead as officers packed into the operations room, shifting in their seats, eyes pinned to the front.

A map of the Big East Hill Section stretched across the corkboard, red circles marking a grim reality: a rising wave of crime and a disturbing surge in missing child alerts.

At the center of it all stood Chief Avery, a mountain of a man, every inch the stereotype: broad-shouldered, square-jawed, uniform stretched tight over sheer authority. His presence alone commanded silence, and when he spoke, his voice cut through the air like a gavel striking the bench.

"Ladies and gentlemen, Mischief Night is upon us," he boomed. "And as we all know, it ain't about trick-or-treating."

A hush fell over the room as the trickle of murmurs ceased.

Chief Avery dragged his fingers across the overlapping circles on the board behind him, tracing the emerging pattern. "The sector's population is increasing. It's putting a strain on our department." His sharp gaze swept across the gathered officers and members of the press hanging on his words. *A puzzle waiting to be solved*, he thought to himself.

From the side of the room, Natalie Dobbs, the department's media liaison, broke the silence.

"Are we talking about the missing kids? Or the ones doing the vandalizing?"

Avery's jaw tightened. He watched the officers shifting in their seats, their faces worn with exhaustion. Stepping forward, he squared his shoulders. The years hung heavy on him, etched into the creases around his eyes and mouth.

"We know this playbook," he said, his voice steady but tinged with frustration. "Every year, kids run wild on Mischief Night, unattended, unsupervised, playing pranks like the streets belong to them."

He let that hang. Then he turned to the board, his brow furrowed, and continued. "But the problem is… while they're out there ringing doorbells, unsupervised revelers turn into predators."

A ripple of murmurs swept through the room. Some officers exchanged glances. Chief Avery waited, letting his words settle.

His voice dropped. Not with weakness, but with gravity. "And while we're spread thin—gang wars spiraling, criminals acting like rabid dogs—we cannot afford to let these kids slip through the cracks."

Chief Avery exhaled, shifting his stance. His hand hovered over the pinned crime scene photos before curling into a fist at his side.

"That's why I need every officer, every detective—hell, even the damn janitor—out there sweeping these streets. The focus is prevention."

One by one, he locked eyes with his officers, making sure they understood: This wasn't just another briefing. This was a mission.

"We don't get to sit back. Not this time. The council just approved the budget for new boots on the ground. Three new detectives. Two men, one woman."

He paused, drawing in a slow breath, the weight of responsibility pressing down on him like concrete poured from above.

"This city's coming apart at the seams. But these kids? They're not part of that war. They are our *future*."

The room held its breath. Avery looked out at his team with tempered affection. When he spoke again, his voice carried the kind of solemn weight that turned orders into purpose.

"I know you're tired. Hell, I'm exhausted. But they need us."

Then, one final command. Simple.

"God bless and pray for the children of the Big East."

There was no applause. No dramatic exhale. Just the quiet understanding that, by the time dawn broke, it might already be too late for some.

The room erupted into motion, officers rising fast, chairs scraping, and boots striking the tile. A wave of urgency was crashing into the city's underbelly.

CHAPTER 1

THEY CALL ME DETECTIVE DAWSON

OCTOBER 31ST – 6:36 AM

The tie came first. Always.

Looped, tightened, adjusted with the precision of a craftsman. My hands- scarred but steady. They moved on instinct. The real engine? That was up top—trained by war, wired by trauma, always calculating. In the mirror, I roved over a face that had seen too much: salt-and-pepper hair, cropped close; beard trimmed just enough to keep the world from thinking I'd given up.

I studied the tetchy movement of my sharp brown eyes. Always scanning. Always seeing. They had watched this city rot, seen the worst it had to offer, and never learned how to look away.

Then, just visible beneath my shirt collar, that telltale flash of chrome. I unplugged the charging cable from my sternum and tapped it for luck, not enough pressure to activate anything.

Behind me stood my apartment: a functional, uncluttered space of distractions. Commendations lined the walls, dust settling over old victories. I rarely acknowledged them. They were just distant applause from a crowd I stopped performing for.

But then my eyes landed on the one thing that still mattered. A yellowed newspaper pinned between the plaques, a screaming headline: "*Veteran Detective Caught Tampering with DNA Evidence.*"

The face beneath the headline wasn't mine. It belonged to a man I once called 'partner'. A man whose betrayal cut deeper than any knife ever could. I twinged, clawing at my chest.

I exhaled slowly. Some wounds don't heal. They just stop bleeding.

I reached for my cologne, let the wood-and-spice scent settle like armor, then pulled on my trench coat. Frayed at the cuffs, worn in like an old habit.

Then, I grabbed my Porsche keys. And the revolver—a .357 Magnum. All black. Grandfathered in through decades of service. Built for war. Carried for justice. Six shots of old-school reckoning.

No safety. No compromises.

Just like me.

Two minutes later, the Porsche slid onto the street, its growl blending with the city's morning frenzy. The police scanner crackled, static filling the cabin, but I wasn't in a hurry just yet. I reached for the dial.

The scanner volume went down. The music pumped up.

A low, slow jazz melody swelled into life, like an urban symphony riding shotgun with me. For a moment, the day breathed. Then—

"We've got a 211 in progress at Parkside Jewelry, 5th and Alston. Any units available?"

Barbara, the voice of the department, was already at her front desk before the sun was up. Her dulcet tone barely registered anymore, just another part of the daily cycle. I kept the music up, fingers tapping the wheel, until…

"Badge 287 checking in for duty."

I heard it, even over the music. Not the words, but the way they were said. A rookie? But good with her speech. Steady. Not stiff, not fumbling. Like she already understood the weight of what she was stepping into.

I turned the music down. Never heard *that* voice before.

Then I shrugged it off.

7:45 AM

Detective Emily Hunter stood before the Big East Police Headquarters, its steel-and-glass façade looming over the city like an unshakable force. This wasn't just a police station; it was the station, a place spoken about in urban legend. An institution forged in blood, sweat, and the relentless pursuit of justice.

Now, it would be her home.

She stepped through the rotary doors, instantly engulfed by the precinct's restless energy. Coffee, sweat, and urgent voices fought their way through the constant click-clack of keyboards and sharp bursts of radio chatter. Ahead, a uniformed officer sat behind a reinforced glass checkpoint, barely glancing up as she approached.

Emily slid her badge under the window. "Detective Emily Hunter. First day. Homicide."

The officer inspected it briefly. "No keycard yet?"

"Not yet."

"Alright. I'll buzz you through."

A mechanical buzz sounded, unlocking the glass doors leading to the elevators.

As she stepped inside and pressed 10, she examined her reflection in the stainless steel doors: a crisp three-piece suit, badge clipped in place, and an unreadable expression. Perfect. She exhaled.

When the doors slid open, she entered a world of controlled chaos. The bullpen pulsed with life—officers escorting perps, detectives deep in conversation, case files stacked in precarious towers. As Emily walked toward the back, she tried to absorb every detail: phones ringing; the particular flavor of coffee in the air; a strung-out suspect slouched in a chair, eyes glassy and distant; a rookie officer struggling with a drunk, the suspect slurring obscenities while being dragged to holding; a mugshot in progress, the detective's voice clipped: "Face forward. Now to the side."

Justice here wasn't clean. It was messy, loud, and relentless. She pushed through the door marked HOMICIDE.

Immediately, the noise dimmed.

Here, the energy was heavier. The walls were lined with cork boards, pinned-up photos, and scrawled notes. Desks were littered with half-empty coffee cups, open files, and stacks of paperwork that looked like they hadn't been touched in days.

Detective Hunter couldn't help but smile. *This was the real work.* She scanned the room, spotting an empty desk. Before she could settle in, a gravelly voice rang out from behind.

"Hey, what's going on?"

She turned, recognizing him from his photo. *Clayton Cash.*

He was stocky, confident, and wearing an easy smirk, his button-up wrinkled as if he'd been pulling doubles since day one. Already standing, he stepped around his desk to greet her.

"Detective Clayton Cash," he said, offering his hand. "Welcome to the trenches."

"Detective Emily Hunter." She shook his hand firmly. "Looks more like a warzone than a trench."

"Same thing, really," Cash chuckled. "Better get used to the mess. Or it'll chew you up and spit you out."

Before she could respond, a loud thud sounded from the next cubicle, followed by a muttered curse, then movement.

Omar Johnston stepped out from behind the partition, stretching like he'd been sitting too long. Lean, sharp-eyed, and carrying the sort of unspoken confidence that suggested he was used to winning, he eyed her.

"So, you're the last newbie." His tone was casual, but with a bite. "Completing our trilogy."

Emily met his gaze without hesitation. "And you must be Johnston."

"That's right." His eyes flicked to Cash, then back to her. "Figured they'd stick me with a rookie cop. Instead, I get to break in a fresh-out-the-wrapper detective."

Emily smirked. "Lucky me, I heard I'm getting paired with someone competent."

Cash let out a low whistle. "Damn. That didn't take long."

"Might as well get used to it," she replied. "I'm full of surprises."

Johnston leaned against the cubicle wall. "We'll see about that."

Cash seemed to sense the unspoken challenge and grinned. "Alright, before you two start measuring badges, let's grab some coffee."

Emily shook her head. "Nah, I'll pass for now. Got a couple of things to handle first."

Johnston laughed. "Blowing us off already?"

"Absolutely." Emily winked. "Wouldn't want to set the wrong expectations."

Cash chuckled, then gestured toward Johnston. "We just got finished moving in."

Johnston nudged his cubicle door, which creaked and groaned, nearly falling off its hinges. "I got stuck with this masterpiece," he muttered. Leaning toward Emily, he whispered, "But you? You got the real prize."

Emily raised an eyebrow. "Oh?"

Johnston tilted his head toward the empty desk next to the biggest one in the room. "Yeah," he smirked. "You're next to Dawson."

Emily's stomach tightened, not with nerves, but with understanding. Charlie Dawson. Her new partner. The name had weight.

Johnston clapped Cash on the shoulder. "But I got my perks. Ain't that right, partner?"

Cash and Johnston exchanged a quick, practiced handshake. When Johnston's eyes flicked back to Emily, she found something unreadable in his gaze, like he wasn't sure he liked her yet.

"Alright," Johnston said, which finally cut the tension. "Coffee's in the back. We'll meet up later."

Cash smirked. "Maybe even grab some food. There's a meeting soon, anyway."

Emily adjusted her badge. "Sure. But first…" She tilted her head. "What time does Dawson usually roll in?"

Johnston snorted. "Don't worry. You'll hear him before you see him."

7:59 AM

The city blurred past, whispering of a place once full of promise. I barely noticed the blacked-out van parked too perfectly along the street, nor the vendor arguing with his customer.

But I did notice *her*.

Kelsey Rose. Six-foot-one, curvy, with a press badge and a habit of being where she shouldn't be. She stood outside the chaos of a fatal wrong-way accident, while patrol cars strobed red and blue against her sharp features.

I turned my head, hoping to slip past unnoticed.

No such luck. She spotted me, then took a step forward and stuck out a leg.

"Oh, *hell* no." Cursing, I swerved just in time to keep from clipping a sedan, nearly causing another pile-up behind me. I hit the brakes, threw it in reverse, and lit up the Porsche's police lights, blocking a lane. Stepping out, I adjusted my trench coat, my badge flashing under the morning sun.

"Move it back, pal." I waved off a lingering driver. Then, to the officer gawking nearby, I yelled, "Hey! Get over here and flag traffic! What are you waiting for, a red carpet?" He scrambled to attention.

I slammed my car door shut and turned to Ms. Rose. "You trying to get me killed or something?"

Kelsey smirked, flipping open her notepad. "It's called stopping traffic, Detective. Something a woman like me tends to do."

I exhaled through my nose. "More like giving insurance companies a reason to raise their rates."

She laughed, tapping the end of her pen against her chin. "Good thing I know a few good cops. Maybe one of them can help me out?"

I crossed my arms, tilting my chin up. "I don't know. Most people know how to avoid unnecessary chaos. But you? You breathe it in like oxygen."

She stepped closer, locking eyes with me. "And yet… You stopped."

I shook my head, smiling despite myself. "Not for you. For the paperwork."

She grinned, already jotting something down. "Don't be so dramatic, Detective. Now, I have a few questions for you."

I sighed, giving her a look. But before she could ask anything, the scanner crackled to life.

"287 responding to the 211. En route."

That voice again. I glanced at the radio, from which the jazz still rhythmically pulsed.

Kelsey noticed. "Something wrong?"

I got back into the Porsche and pulled the door shut, the seat leather creaking beneath my weight. A moment passed, where I could feel her eyes on me through the glass.

I rolled the window down slowly. The city noise slipped back in, but it was nothing compared to the silence stretching between us.

She didn't look away. Not once.

The answer came out as smooth as I could muster. "Nothing I can't handle." I revved the engine, the well-tuned exhaust ripping through the air as I pulled away. In the rearview mirror, Kelsey still stood there, not a single ounce of determination lost.

En route to the precinct, the Porsche hugged the pavement, slicing through traffic like a blade. Another buzz from the center console. Another missed call. Someone wanted my time—time that belonged elsewhere.

The job always came first.

Gradually, the city yawned awake. OPEN signs flickered on. Street vendors prepped their stands. A kid on a BMX weaved through traffic like he had nine lives.

I had none of that energy. A dull headache throbbed at the base of my skull, the kind that came from too many hours buried in case files paired with too little sleep. I needed coffee—real coffee, not the watered-down excuse for wake-up juice waiting for me at the station. But time was already working against me.

The police scanner continued to crackle with background noise, the city reporting in on itself.

"Unit 5, 10-54 at East 130th. Possible DUI."

"Dispatch, we got another stolen vehicle, a blacked-out Chevy, no plates. Spotted near Prospect."

Just another morning in the trenches.

My phone buzzed. Avery.

I sighed and pressed the button. "What's up, Chief?"

"Dawson, where the hell are you? We're waiting."

I glanced at the clock. 8:42. Lineup was at 8:30. "I'm on my way."

Avery scoffed. *"You mean 'late', like usual."*

I smirked but tried to keep it out of my voice. "Well, Chief, I was out here doing the job your patrolmen should be handling. Damn near started directing traffic."

"Funny. So, I assume you already heard the rumors, even though you conveniently skipped the meeting?"

"I hear a lot of rumors."

"Well, this one's real. The city finally approved the budget. Forty new uniforms, fifteen replacements, and three new detectives."

"I saw the names."

"Then you know what's coming."

———

I didn't answer.

Avery let the silence hang. *"Let's just say… You might be breaking in some new blood."*

I exhaled through my nose. "I don't do mentoring."

"You do now." Click.

The call cut out.I drummed my fingers against the steering wheel, eyes flicking to the rearview mirror. My reflection stared back., Fine. Three new detectives. If I got my space, I didn't care. I grabbed my phone and started looking them up again:

Omar Johnson. Clayton Cash. Emily Hunter.

Their faces stared back at me, too young, too eager, too much social media presence. How the hell can you be a detective but still leave traces of digital footprints, gym selfies, and street fair pics?

I shook my head, flicking the screen off. I rolled up to The Big East Police Department, standing tall against the city skyline, glass reflecting the morning light. This place had history; it was a house built on the backs of the detectives who came before me, where cases were solved, lives were ruined, and the job never truly ended.

The lot was already packed, patrol cars and unmarked units lined up in neat rows. I pulled in, killed the engine, and stepped out.

Outside, the air smelled of fresh asphalt. Ahead, a pair of uniforms escorted a perp toward a transport van. The guy was fresh off the street: bloody lip, one shoe missing, wrist shackles too tight. He shuffled forward in a fluorescent jumpsuit marked *IN PROCESSING*.

A detective leaned against the van, arms crossed. "See, Dawson?" he shouted at me as I passed. "This is what happens when you're late. You miss all the fun."

I kept walking. "Fun, huh? Looks like you did me a favor."

The perp blinked up at me through swollen eyes, mumbling, "He compensatin'… for sumthin'."

I barely glanced at him. "Yeah. For your sentencing."

The detective barked a laugh as he slammed the van door shut on the guy.

The station doors yawned open, swallowing me into the chaos. I winced at the abrasive sound of phones ringing, paperwork being slapped onto desks, and everyone's collective caffeine-fueled anxiety. I registered the usual glances as I moved through the lobby, some nods, some stares.

I hit the elevator button. Swiped my badge. Boarded when it arrived.

Up to the 10th floor. To Barbara. To lineup.

To whatever fresh headache Avery just dropped in my lap.

The elevator doors slid open, and the station hit me in waves—oily takeout, printer toner, perspiration. *The morning rush.* The 10th floor of Big EPD churned like a beast that never stopped breathing. The brass had tried modernizing it—glass partitions, sleek desks, updated computers—but the bones stayed the same.

Mahogany doors lined the halls, relics from a bygone era when detectives smoked indoors and slammed perps into filing cabinets. The walls were crowded with yellowing newspapers and framed commendations, reminders of the cases that had built this department.

But prestige didn't solve murders.

Straight ahead, Barbara. She had already spied me over her glasses, her desk planted at the front like a sentry post, a one-woman firewall between the outside world and the madness within.

"Hey, Barb. How's everything?"

She barely looked up. "It's Monday, Dawson. How do you think it is?"

I smiled. "The start of another beautiful week in The Big East."

She exhaled, sliding a stack of mail toward me. "This came in for you."

I flipped through case reports, complaints, and standard bureaucratic trash until something stood out. A folder, tucked between the newspapers, marked: *FOR DETECTIVE DAWSON – HAND DELIVERY ONLY.*

I arched a brow. "Who sent this?"

"James."

Great.

———

James was our resident CSI whiz—top of his class, fast-tracked into forensics. He'd been a street cop before they stashed him away in a lab, solving murders with algorithms and tech that barely seemed legal.

I tucked the file under my arm. "Do me a favor. Hold my calls. Anything important, dump it onto my ex-partner's voicemail. Once that fills up, start passing them off to the rookies."

Barbara smirked. "Sink or swim?"

I shrugged. "Only one way to find out." I headed down the main corridor, past the maze of glass offices and open desks, my boots echoing against the tile.

Unlike the chiefs locked away in their smoked-glass offices, signing papers and watching from a safe distance, I sat in the thick of it. Some of these guys? They'd been promoted straight into chairs. Typing reports, pushing policies, acting like Geppetto pulling strings in a department full of puppets. They'd been doing it so long, I was surprised they didn't all have carpal tunnel.

Me? I put my scars to work. My desk sat in the middle of the bullpen, close enough to hear the noise, far enough to keep my space. I'd solved more cases from that chair than most detectives had in their entire careers.

The real detective work happens in the middle of it all—amongst the chaos and confusion and a collective of clues. You sit, you listen, you pick up on things the others miss.

A voice rang out, sharp, desperate. "I didn't do it!"

To my left, a camera flash popped. Another perp getting processed—handcuffed, wide-eyed, already rehearsing his defense.

I threw another look over at the bullpen, teeming with activity.

Then, I saw them. The new blood. They stood near the back of the bullpen, waiting.

First, Clayton Cash.

Jesus, the guy looked nothing like his file photo. In the academy picture, he'd been lean, squared up, the kind of recruit they put on brochures. Now? I had no idea how this guy passed the physical. I kept walking.

Next up, Omar Johnston. Short. Stocky. Built like a damn fire hydrant. Five-foot-seven but standing like he was six-four. I could already tell he was going to be a handful from the way his jaw stayed locked and his arms folded tight. Some guys carried tension in their shoulders. Johnston carried it in his whole damn DNA. I'd been doing this long enough to read people fast: who was cocky, who was nervous, who was running off pure adrenaline. Johnston? He looked permanently pissed off.

Cash stepped toward me, then Johnston. Then, out of my right-side peripheral, she appeared. I looked down.

Badge 287. Emily Hunter.

Just like I thought. Blonde. Blue eyes. Five-seven. The kind of polished, clean-cut look that screamed 'academy'.

She wasn't tense, but she wasn't relaxed either. Something was calculating behind her eyes, like she was already taking mental notes, analyzing the room. From the other two, I got it—that 'starstruck' vibe. But her? That'd take some sorting out.

I frowned away. "Listen, I'm just a guy who puts in the hours. Don't make it weird."

I could see Hunter looking like she had something to say. I kept talking before she got the chance.

"Alright. We're going to start slow," I said, scanning all three of them. "None of this, '*throw 'em in the fire*' bullshit. You'll be pulling CVs, working the backlog, and getting familiar with the system. I don't need dead weight around the station."

They nodded a little too fast, the need to prove themselves shining in their eyes. I exhaled.

The other two peeled off, heading to their cubicles, leaving me mercifully to make my way to my desk.

Then, it came.

"Detective Dawson, I've heard so many good things about you."

Something about the way she said it—smooth, expertly casual, like she'd practiced it once or twice this morning—made me halt mid-step. I turned around.

Hunter stood there, arms loosely crossed, studying me. "I've gone over your arrest record," she continued, tilting her head. "Your casework is impressive."

I smirked. "Yeah? Well, I do what I can." Then I leaned in slightly. Not too much, just to see how quickly she'd adjust. "Hunter, I presume? Or should I call you Miss Lobel?"

That hit. *A flicker.* Barely there, but I caught it—the quick shift in her expression before she smoothed it over with her own smirk.

"That's a basic search, Dawson," she said, unfazed. "Anybody could pick that up. I could get that off LinkedIn."

I shrugged. "Sure. But now we have to dig into the real stuff. And that? That's not going to be online."

———

She crossed her arms more tightly. "Oh? And where are you going to find it?"

I met her stare. "Where it actually matters."

For a second, she didn't respond. Then, she let out the smallest chuckle, as if to let me know she wasn't rattled. "You sure you want to start this?" she asked. "I'd hate for our first conversation to end with you realizing I can keep up."

Alright. So, we had one of these. She'd do fine with paperwork. "What do you pack?" I asked.

".45 ACP," she said, brushing her hip. Without hesitation, she unholstered the weapon and offered it up for inspection.

Not bad. Compact, clean. Nothing like my battered revolver that had seen more than its fair share of action.

I raised an eyebrow. "Small, but solid." I gave a low chuckle. "You name it yet?"

She grinned. "Sasha Fierce. Judge, jury, executioner."

I rolled my eyes. "Oh great, you give it gender pronouns, too?"

The grin slipped just for a half-second. "Yeah," she said, voice steady. "And for the record, I graduated top of my class, led an all-male unit, and was named Female Marksman of the Year in 2009. I didn't 'sleep my way to the top', if that's what you're going to insinuate that next."

I shook my head. "I wasn't. But thanks for putting that out there."

She folded her arms, posture stiff with intent. "Then you should already know—I didn't come here to blend in."

I sat down in the middle of the bullpen like it was my living room

And there her bag was on a desk, too close to mine.

Not an accident. Not with her.

She wasn't just testing the waters—she was checking the temperature.

A look in her eye that said she either knew something I didn't or wanted me to think she did.

Polished. Poised. Like someone who'd rehearsed walking into a room she wasn't invited to.

I cleared my throat, just loud enough. "Look, you can post up wherever you want. But I'm a bullpen detective. I don't hide in glass offices. I don't sneak around the back. I'm front and center. Always have been."

No response. Just that same steady stare, like she was measuring me.

Then I continued Cain was the last straw. Whatever this was—it better not be round two.

Chief Avery lumbered into the room. He cut through the bullpen like a warhead with a badge, barking orders, brushing off greetings: all business. The room seemed to straighten up just from the weight of his presence.

His eyes locked on me and Hunter.

"Well, well," he said, slowing his pace at my desk. "I see Dawson hasn't chewed your head off yet, Hunter. Miracles do happen."

I stayed quiet. She didn't.

"Give him time," she shot back.

He cracked a small grin. The tension settled a bit before he snapped it back tight. "Dawson. Hunter. My office. Now."

I glanced at her, then back toward the office door, and exhaled through my nose. *This was about to be a problem.* Avery's door creaked open, and we followed him in together.

While the phones continued to ring outside, inside, the Chief's office was a fortress of case files and bad decisions. The air was different—thick with old smoke, dust, and quiet command. Commendation plaques lined the walls like battleground flags. His desk looked like it hadn't been cleared since the last riot.

Avery didn't waste time. He tossed a file onto his desk. "Three kids. Same time. Same night. Missing." The Chief barely looked up as he slid the stack of files across the desk. "This is your caseload."

I flipped open the first folder and scanned it: Lucas Bennett, Oliver Ferguson, Jacob Smith. Mischief Night. *Of course.*

The Chief kept talking. "You're also assigned to last year's Mischief Night cases, maybe you can drum up a pattern. I suggest you and your team start there."

I blinked. "Wait a minute. My team?"

"Your team," the Chief repeated, with obvious satisfaction.

I snapped the folder shut with a flick of my wrist. "I don't mind having rookies on the team, but they're not ready for these crimes."

The Chief leaned back, unimpressed. "That's why it's called on-the-job training. Also, Hunter is your partner."

A rookie partner with a novice team in the most dangerous sector… *Did I just hear him right?*

Avery turned to Hunter. "Since your partner decided to skip the briefing, let me fill you in. Some parts call it 'Knock, Knock, Ginger.'"

Hunter frowned. "Knock, Knock, Ginger?"

"Old prank. Kids knock on doors, ring bells, and run before anyone answers. It used to be harmless. Now? They go missing instead."

I clicked my tongue. "Cute. So, what, we get an official 'Ding Dong Vanished' report now?"

Avery didn't blink. "Make jokes all you want, but this isn't just another missing persons case. Something is off. Three kids. Gone. No solid contact in days." Avery shook his head with apparent exhaustion. "We're escalating this to a Mischief Alert."

I sighed, grabbing the file. "Fine. But add it to the list of other things I do around here."

Avery shot me a dry look. "You want a medal?"

Hunter, ignoring our bickering, flipped through the first few pages. "How do we know they're really missing? What if they're just skipping?"

Avery shook his head. "Parents thought they were skipping school. The school thought they were home sick. Nobody kept track." He paused and looked at me, then at her. "Hunter, can Dawson and I talk for a moment?"

She hesitated before stepping out. I waited till her silhouette reappeared behind the smoked glass, as did Avery.

He leaned in closer to me. "Dawson, you were once in her shoes. Young. Eager. And this job is risky. There's no getting around that."

I scoffed. "Oh, great. So now I'm a babysitter."

"She's a young rookie, Dawson. A detective, ready to make her mark."

43

I leaned back, exhaling slowly. "Well, looks like I don't have a choice. But if I'm stuck with this, I'm making a lot of special requests."

Avery sighed. "Yeah, I figured."

I stood, adjusting my suit. "Since I'm officially the department's chaperone, I suppose I'll start by putting these rookies to the test."

Avery crossed his arms. "You mean train them, right?"

I grinned. "Yeah. Train them. Shooting drills. Tactical maneuvers. Maybe a little wiretapping."

Avery cut me off. "*Wiretapping?* Charlie, don't you go tapping lines without a warrant."

I grinned wider. "Oh yeah? And what are you going to do? Demote me?"

Avery shifted in his seat, rubbing his temples. He thought he had won the battle, but now I was the one making demands.

"Look, Chief, I don't have time to run through the bureaucracy of The Big East. We need to hit the ground running. You want these kids to shine, don't you?"

Avery grumbled. "Yeah, but we also want to follow protocol. We're detectives, not cowboys."

"Yeah, yeah. So, while we're at it, we'll need that new SWAT vehicle—the one you didn't give me last year."

Avery scoffed. "No." As expected. He sighed, rubbing his temples even harder. Reflexively, he looked at my sternum before pulling his gaze back up to eye level. "Anything else?"

I pulled the door open, letting the moment breathe before tossing a smirk over my shoulder. *For you?*

"Not even a Christmas card."

And finally—*finally*—I got my damn coffee.

CHAPTER 2

RAISED BY THE BLOCK

NOVEMBER 3RD – 11:14 PM

Moonlight cut through the autumn darkness, silver beams slicing across graffiti-stained walls. The old, sagging couch in the corner barely held its shape, offering little comfort as Kordell leaned back, arms crossed, watching his crew.

The room reeked of cheap weed, sweat, and the lingering scent of last night's liquor—the usual cocktail of their existence. A TV in the corner played something nobody was watching, the low static blending into the hum of downtown life outside.

Across from Kordell, J-Rock and Taurese sat, their hoods up, hands buried deep in their pockets. J-Rock's eyes were empty as he stared into the distance, his recent losses seeming to weigh on him.

Kordell's voice was low, steady as an anchor in a storm. "How you holding up, man?"

Taurese exhaled, barely shaking his head. "It's rough, Kordell."

Kordell nodded, knowing there weren't any words that could fix it. "Family is family, right?"

"Damn straight." Taurese's voice was resonant with grief but firm. No matter what happened, they stuck together. That's what this was.

In the background, Clink sat near the window, lighting and extinguishing a cigarette lighter with a soft *click-click-click*. The flame bounced off his features in brief flickers of orange. He wasn't part of the serious talk—not his style—but he was listening.

"Life's a real bitch," Clink muttered, smirking, though his eyes reflected the same exhaustion that hung in the room.

Kordell rubbed his jaw, the weight of leadership pressing on him more than usual. "Be strong, brother. We're here for you."

Clink snorted, letting the lighter snap shut. "Yeah, yeah, we all got love for each other and shit. Ain't nobody dropping no tears, though. Right, T?"

For a moment, there was peace. Until Clink shattered it like glass.

"Yo, yo, yo!" Clink's voice suddenly boomed through the room. He flashed a grin. "Nearly forgot. Y'all won't believe what I pulled off today."

Kordell rolled his eyes. "This better not be another one of your dumbass stunts."

Clink ignored him, launching into his story with gangster flair. "Man, I was out on Bay Street, saw this lady walking all slow and sad with a big-ass purse. I mean, it was *calling* me. So, what'd I do?"

Taurese arched his brow, leaning forward. "Don't tell me…"

"Snatched that shit and took off like a Heisman, man!" Clink laughed, motioning like he was stiff-arming an invisible defender. "I hit a cut so fast, I could've gone to college on a full-ride scholarship the way I was moving."

Kordell's jaw tightened. His patience was running thinner by the second. "You went too far this time." His voice was flat yet sharp. "The OGs wanna talk. And I ain't saving your ass this time."

Clink's grin faltered for a second before he forced it back. "Man, the OGs can stay worried about me. I'm like their favorite soap opera."

Kordell didn't flinch. "They ain't entertained no more."

A silence settled between them. Then, Kordell leaned forward, his voice colder now. "You remember, Lil JJ, don't ya ?"

Clink's smirk faded. Taurese looked away.

Kordell's eyes stayed locked on him. "Last person JJ saw before he disappeared? A white dude. Near the Ville."

Clink shifted in his seat. He knew where this was going.

Kordell rubbed his chin, his voice turning razor sharp. "Lil JJ was loud. Reckless. He thought nobody could touch him."

Taurese exhaled. "You think that's why he got clipped?"

Kordell leaned forward. "The night he disappeared, somebody saw him looking shook near the cut behind Tom Caldwell's place. Like he saw something he wasn't supposed to."

Taurese's expression soured. "Are you certain?"

Kordell reached into his hoodie pocket and pulled out a broken dog tag chain stained with dried blood. The tag, however, was missing.

Clink tensed up. "Where'd you find that?"

Kordell didn't blink. "Near Tom's crib. Bushes were trampled. Like somebody fought back before they got taken."

Clink cleared his throat. "You call the OGs yet?"

Kordell shot back, "You tell the OGs—why we ain't move on him ourselves yet?"

He let the words hang like gun smoke.

"We ain't passin' off our problems.

We F-N-O. Fear no one."

Clink leaned forward, gassing it up.

"Yeah—and soon as nightfall hits, we light up his porch."

J-Rock nodded hard, heat in his chest.

"Aight then, let's move. We ain't gotta wait—"

Kordell's hand cut through the air—clean, sharp. The room froze.

"Nah. Not with Big East cops already circlin'. We just now settin' up this money play. Nothing screws that up."

Heads dipped in tight, silent nods of acknowledgment.

Clink cleared his throat.

"So… what's the play?"

Kordell's gaze swept the room.

"We ain't movin' sloppy. From now on, nobody rolls solo. Double up every time you step foot in that district."

J-Rock muttered, still hot.

"Man, we—"

Kordell cut him off again, voice like steel.

"Two deep, always. One carries, and one clean. If it jumps off, the one strapped takes the charge.

J-Rock still looked unconvinced, but he said nothing. Taurese shined the barrel of his gun, not saying a word

The room fell silent again. Three kids from the neighborhood, who had survived the streets thus far and joined a gang—a family, in a world that hadn't given them a chance.

A world that had already chosen its winners and losers.

A world where the code kept them breathing, but only for as long as they followed it.

Kordell glanced down at the dog tag, still caked with dried old blood. The Bible said vengeance belonged to the Lord. But out here? Sometimes, God worked through men, and Kordell was ready to be His instrument.

CHAPTER 3

THE ROOKIE STANDOFF

NOVEMBER 3RD – 10:10 AM

Arriving at the shooting range, I could hear the soft echoes of distant gunfire, a constant murmur in the background. The real action, however, was unfolding two levels below, hidden behind layers of concrete and steel.

I pulled up and stepped out of my car, adjusting my jacket shoulder-holster with practiced ease.

Some men show up. Me? *I arrive.*

Across the lot, Johnston was bent over again, struggling with his laces.

"Always with the damn laces," I muttered under my breath. I strolled toward him, letting my shadow fall across him first. "What's the deal, Johnston? Fashion statement or battlefield prep?"

Without looking up, he murmured, "Shooters got to have a secure fit, boss. Can't have laces coming undone in a firefight."

Smartass.

I opened my mouth to fire back when Hunter's voice sliced through the tension.

"*Morning,* Johnston," she said, her tone plain but cutting.

I turned just enough to catch Johnston's reaction. He stiffened. The vestiges of some previous standoff that had clearly left a mark. Good. Let it burn. I stayed silent, watching them circle one another like vultures.

With relish, I realized this might break before it even comes together. Transfers. Reassignments. I'd seen it all before, internal conflicts escalating until someone got pulled out, moved to a different division, or stuck behind a desk. Tension like that didn't need much fuel. Just a push. And if it came to that? I'd be back on the streets solo. *Funny how things turn out...*

Before it could boil over, Cash strode in, big presence, bigger voice. Now we had a crowd.

"Hey, peace, what's happening? Are we throwing hands or throwing lead?"

I cut in. "First things first." I looked at him and asked, "Did you bring what I asked for?"

Cash grinned and slid the rolled-up enlarged photo from under his arm, like he'd been guarding it all morning. "Hot off the press."

I took it from him, unrolling it carefully, keeping it tilted just out of Johnston and Hunter's line of sight. They were in a slow-motion grudge match. No need to add more friction.

And there it was. A grainy, blown-up photo of my niece, Sandra… and him.

Mr. Probation.

That's what I called him, anyway. Not to his face, of course. Didn't want to tip him off if he ever went missing.

There's always that one guy, the one your niece or daughter brings home who shouldn't be allowed within ten feet of your family name.

And now? She's a cop somewhere. Just landed her lead position. Finally doing something that matters.

And *this* is who she picks to bring around? Unbelievable.

I folded the photo and slid it into my inner jacket pocket like it was evidence, then gave Cash a nod. "Job well done," I said, shaking his hand. "First mission complete: You printed something."

He chuckled. Clueless. Hunter crossed her arms. Johnston didn't even blink.

I turned back to Johnston and Hunter, still sizing each other up. "Alright. Talk's over. Time to shoot."

I hit the buzzer at the entrance. *Click.* The steel doors unlocked.

This was Chris's Armory. Nothing like the department range. This was where the elite trained. Breath control. Sharp aim and no second chances

We passed rows of high-end tactical gear snipers, riot shields gleaming beneath the sterile flicker of fluorescents.

Another buzzer. Another heavy click. We stepped down into the underground range. At the bottom, I flicked the lights on one by one until the place woke up, metal, concrete, and violence in the air.

I smirked, watching Cash's face finally catch on to why I had him print the photo. *Message received.*

At the booths, I handed out gear. "One thing I am? Reckless. But I'm also big on safety." I passed out three pairs of safety glasses. "Here's your Eye Pro."

They slipped them on. Next, earmuffs.

"I hate seeing young detectives with hearing aids. Messes with the whole tough-guy image."

Johnston's lip twitched. Almost a laugh. Close enough.

"Let me get lanes one, three, and six," I barked at the attendant in the booth.

Cash raised an eyebrow. I handed him back the enlarged photo.

"Put this in lane one."

Johnston and Hunter's targets were set. The buzzer stood poised. I let the silence hang, tense, electric.

Then, I snapped.

"It's DOUBLE TAP TUESDAY!"

The words cracked through the bunker like thunder.

"Two to the chest, one to the head! This ain't a game! This ain't for play! You wanna sit and push pencils? Or do you wanna be out on the streets *with me*?" I pounded my chest.

"The big dawg."

I started pacing, hands clasped behind my back. "Who's gonna be my marksman? Who's gonna be my guy? Who can I trust when the streets get ugly?" Johnston moved to touch his weapon first. I cut him down instantly. "What are we doing? No practice shots in the streets! No warm-ups! Precision, off the rip!"

Johnston hesitated. "Alright, Capt," he muttered.

I watched him recover from that minor stumble as the light began to change: *Red. Click. Yellow. Click. Green.*

Buzzer.

Gunfire erupted. Cash and I stalked behind them, watching everything.

Johnston? Not bad. He had rhythm. Steady. Reliable.

But Hunter? She had the *flow.*

I barked over the firestorm, voice slicing through like a blade. "Who's my marksman? Who's gonna be my eagle eye?"

They didn't even flinch. Gunshots kept exploding. They couldn't hear me.

Good. That was the point.

Locked in.

Round one ended. They reloaded. I could've ended it right there.

But nah, I let the tension *simmer. As a Second set of targets zipped downrange.*

"Can't just let it kick off like this," I muttered. "Let 'em go again."

Round two.

Buzzer.

Gunfire exploded again. Casings hit the floor, ricocheting off steel like angry popcorn.

Once it was over, it didn't take long to tally the groupings. I just stared at the targets in my hands.

And I thought: Should I boost morale around this dump? Give them something to hold onto?

Or should I *shatter* them?

Like a pawn shop TV in a drunken rage. Like a promises-to-quit letter crumpled in a junkie's back pocket. Like a… well, you get the point.

All of a sudden, I snapped back to the moment. I looked down at the four bullet-riddled sheets. Two shooters, two rounds each. Guess it was time to announce a winner.

Me being Dawson… what do you *think* I said? I announced, dry as ever, "If I had to bet my life on one of you in a real firefight, I'd start writing my will."

I spat on the floor. "But since I must… Hunter."

Johnston stiffened. That was a clean hit to his ego. I tossed the papers at them. "Hang that up on your fridge."

The team started filing out. But Cash? He stayed behind.

I turned to lane one, where the enlarged photo of my niece and her sketchy boyfriend hung. I thought it was just me, the gun, and the image.

Sandra.

Her boyfriend.

His face smug, cocky, like he thought he mattered.

Hers, untouched. *Always* untouched.

I exhaled slowly. The weight of the revolver rested snug in my shoulder-holster, waiting.

I didn't think. I *moved.*

Cross-body draw. Smooth. Clean.

Spun the cylinder once, twice, caught it mid-air.

Six shots: *BANG. BANG. BANG. BANG. BANG. BANG.* Each round landed exactly where I wanted it.

The gunpowder smell of the range filled my nostrils. My heart hammered a furious rhythm inside my chest.

The motor whined, pulling the target back toward me, inch by inch, closing the distance.

His eyes? Gone. No soul left to stare back.

See, sometimes, the weight of the badge felt like an anchor around my neck. Would I ever be unleashed?

I slid the revolver back into the shoulder-holster, turned, and walked out. I was in another mode.

More determined than ever.

CHAPTER 4

FOUR WALLS, NO MERCY

OCTOBER 31ST – 5:32 AM

Lucas's heart pounded against his ribcage, each beat a terrifying reminder that he was, in fact, alive. His breath came in shallow, uneven bursts as his vision swam. His eyelids fluttered open to a dimly lit room where the burgeoning daylight struggled to pierce through tattered curtains. Blinking slowly, he tried to assemble the scattered fragments of his thoughts. Where am I?

The air was oppressive, pushing in on him like wet sandbags. His eyes landed on a cast iron radiator beneath the window, its dull surface catching what little light crept through.

He pushed himself upright, wincing as pain spiked through his skull. A relentless throb pulsed behind his eyes, but something else quickly seized his attention: a blinking red sensor mounted high in the corner.

It felt out of place, stark against the room's otherwise mundane neglect. A chill crept up his spine.

Lucas's legs trembled beneath him as he staggered to his feet, his gaze darting. Instinctively, his hand shot to his neck. The skin was raw and tender to the touch, and the contact made him recoil.

"What the hell happened?" he whispered, voice fraying at the edges. He prodded the tender area again, but no explanation came. Only pain.

After a moment, the room came into clearer focus, and with it, something far more disturbing: It was a child's bedroom, with a small bed dressed in faded cartoon-print sheets, toys strewn across the floor.

Panic rose anew, sharp and unrelenting. "What is this place?" he mumbled, barely louder than a breath, his pulse now roaring in his ears.

He lunged toward the door, palms slamming against the cold wood as he twisted the knob. He yanked it with all the force he could muster.

"Is anybody there?" he cried. Silence answered. He tried again and again, but nothing broke the stillness. The quiet was suffocating, as though the house were buried deep in forgotten space, sealed off from the world.

Frantic now, Lucas scanned the room for anything—*anything*—he could use as a weapon. But it was a child's space. Innocent, soft... eerie.

Then his eyes caught on the walls. His breath hitched.

Drawings. Dozens of them. Crayon scrawls layered across peeling wallpaper in wild, looping lines. The chaos felt deliberate. Among them, a single photo pinned at eye level froze him… A young boy stared out, no older than ten, dirty-blond-haired, brown-eyed—features that mirrored his own almost exactly.

The air turned colder. Lucas reached out, fingers trembling as they grazed the edge of the photo.

"Is this… supposed to be me?" he whispered. The longer he stared, the deeper the dread sank.

His gaze drifted to a desk in the corner, cluttered with faded photos and yellowed newspaper clippings. Slowly, as though walking through stagnant water, Lucas approached.

With unsteady hands, he sifted through the papers.

Child after child.

Face after face.

Each one bearing the same uncanny resemblance.

"Who are they?" he muttered, voice cracking. "Why do they look like me?"

His stomach twisted. He clutched the desk for balance as the room began to spin.

Then, suddenly, a sound sliced through the stillness—a floorboard creaked behind him. Lucas spun, heart hammering in his chest, eyes darting across every shadowy corner, searching for any sign of movement.

"Is someone there?" he rasped, his voice hoarse with fear. The room seemed to breathe with him: the low hum of the radiator, the rustle of curtains, each noise oppressive, closing in on him…

He strained his ears, listening for any other sound, but only the suffocating silence returned. Instinctively, his trembling hand reached into his pocket for his phone… but then he remembered, he had left it at home. The thing was useless without Wi-Fi anyway.

It all came flooding back: Oliver. Mischief Night. Climbing the hill to the old, abandoned house…

A wave of cold dread swept over him. He felt… stranded, as though the house itself was intent on swallowing him whole.

"Please…" he whispered, the word choking him. "Somebody… anybody." His vision blurred as tears stung his eyes. But he blinked hard, forcing them back. No. He couldn't break now. Not here. Not like this.

Lucas ran a shaky hand down his face, brushing away the few stray tears that had escaped. The spark inside him, fragile but growing, flickered back to life.

Refocusing on the room, he studied every inch, every shadow. *There has to be a way out.* He needed to find it.

He moved cautiously, each step taken with silent prayer. Who had locked him in? And why?

One thing was certain: He wouldn't be consumed by this place. *He would escape, no matter what it took*

CHAPTER 5

SIGNS OF THE STOLEN

NOVEMBER 5TH – 12:31 PM

We found ourselves in the middle of town, in the middle of a storm. Not the weather kind—the kind that brews inside a house when a kid goes missing.

Hunter and I stepped up to the front door of the Bennett's home—a quiet place. Lower-middle-class, just holding on. I knocked, and when the door opened, I saw it immediately: divorce.

Pictures decorated the wall—Lucas with his mother, Lucas with his father. But never all three. Separate frames. Separate lives.

Mrs. Bennett was the one who let us in, gripping a tissue like she could wring answers out of it. Mr. Bennett was already inside, standing stiff by the fireplace, jaw tight like he'd been forced into being here.

Messy. That's what this was.

Hunter took the lead, keeping her voice steady. "We're sorry to intrude, but we need to ask a few questions. Every detail helps."

Mrs. Bennett nodded, eyes red-rimmed. "Anything to bring him home."

Mr. Bennett huffed, crossing his arms. He didn't look at me. He looked at her. Like they were still in court, quibbling over custody arrangements.

Hunter began, "So, Lucas went out with his friends five nights ago…"

Mrs. Bennet nodded. "Jake and Oliver…maybe one or two other kids. He doesn't hang with many." She rubbed her arm, thinking. "I'm not even sure who he left with that night."

I continue to scan the room—family photos, school portraits, a fading science fair ribbon stuck to the fridge. It was a house still trying to hold on to normal. But the cracks were starting to show.

"So, any history of him just… taking off?" I asked. "Skipping school, pulling Mischief Night-type stunts?"

Mr. Bennet let out a sharp breath, arms crossed tight. Mrs. Bennet hesitated, then shook her head. "Not like this."

The air hung heavy.

Then Hunter stepped back in, quiet but focused. She handed me her phone without saying a word.

"Truancy officer marked Jake present this morning," she said. "But I just got a message from one of the teachers—he never showed up to lunch."

I studied the screen for half a beat. "He must've dipped out."

I pulled up my radio. "Put me through to Unit Nine. I want someone on that school building. If he circles back—I want to know."

Just then, Mrs. Bennet's eyes drifted across the room. She locked onto a photo—her and Lucas at a lake, arms wrapped around each other, both smiling like the world was still intact. Her lips parted. And then it hit her.

She shook her head, voice cracking under the weight: "He's always been too curious for his own good."

Interesting.

Hunter pressed on. "Any trouble at school?"

"Nothing we didn't tell you people over the phone last week," Mr. Bennett snapped.

A flicker of hesitation from Mrs. Bennett. Then she said, "There was an issue with bullies a few months back, but the school assured us it was handled."

I glanced at Mr. Bennett. "You agree?"

His jaw twitched. "I wasn't there."

That said plenty. I exhaled. "We'll do everything in our power to bring him home."

Neither of them spoke as Hunter and I headed upstairs.

Lucas's room was neat. Organized. Books on the shelf, telescope by the window. But my eyes went to the wall first.

A *hole*. Like someone had rammed their fist through it. I ran my fingers over the cracked drywall. "Kid's got a temper," I muttered. "Or someone lost theirs on him."

Hunter was already at the desk, flipping through drawers. "Nothing out of place," she murmured, moving methodically.

I spotted something on the nightstand: a phone, face down. I picked it up and turned it over.

Cracked screen. It wouldn't power on.

Hunter looked up. "Why didn't his parents mention he left his phone here? What kid does that?"

I shook my head. "Let's check his computer. Maybe we can see if the data's synced."

Hunter turned on the computer tower, and the screen lit up. With a few taps, Lucas's digital universe emerged: science fair projects, photos with friends, typical childhood stuff. Then—

"Sir," Hunter said, voice tightening. "I think I've got something."

I positioned myself beside her, facing the screen. She scrolled through a conversation thread, which started off casually. However, the messages got more and more concerning. The most recent ones sent my stomach into a lurch.

The screen's glow flashed across our faces as we watched stream after stream. Lucas's search history unraveled—prank videos, reckless stunts, setting fires on porches. A kid drawn to trouble, pushing limits just to see what would happen.

"Good work," I muttered. "That's a lead we can't ignore."

Hunter grabbed her phone and snapped a picture of Lucas's face on the screen. "I'll send this to James, get it run through traffic cams."

I nodded, but my eyes lingered on the room. The walls. The broken phone. The hole in the drywall.

I'd seen this too many times. Parents scrambling to understand. Kids who'd been slipping away, long before they vanished.

It never got easier… And that's when I saw her outside the window, in the driveway.

Kelsey Rose. Already setting up.

Our eyes met. Of *course* she was here. She lived and died by the police scanner. My type of chick, honestly—while everyone else is out dating, she's tailing detectives through the city, chasing heat.

Kelsey caught my eye and gestured towards me, while her cameraman aimed the camera upward. Either she wanted her story, or she wanted me. I headed downstairs, then out onto the front lawn.

"Detective Dawson," Kelsey said, mic live. "Any hints on the missing kids?"

I took a breath. Kept it clean. Kept it sharp. "Me and my department—and I'm proud to say Chief Avery included—we don't wait for no forty-eight or seventy-two-hour windows. Soon as we get even an inclination a child might be missing, we move. Immediately. Our practices are proactive. That's our standard."

Out of the corner of my eye, I spotted him—the Alderman. Creeping up like he belonged in the frame. Like always.

Capello only showed up when the cameras did. He was one of those guys who came to wave, not work. To point fingers, but never to offer solutions. He was quick to criticize you about what you should've done but refused to lift a damn hand for his constituents.

But hey—he was harmless, right?. Until I started digging into his background. That's when the skeletons started showing up, when the favors got called in.

Chapstick politics, they called it. Kissin' ass like it's oxygen.

I turned back to Kelsey, decided to flip the script a little, just to keep her guessing.

I looked right into the camera. "And big thanks to Miss Kelsey Rose—following me around like a shadow. Who knows? If this keeps up, we might just launch a daily show together. 'Crime Watch with Kelsey', airing right after rush hour."

Her crew chuckled. She tried not to blush. Failed.

"For the viewers," I added, pointing at the lens, "if you got tips, send 'em straight to Kelsey. She's on it like clockwork."

I turned, ready to walk out of shot, camera still rolling.

And just like that—boom. Capello slid up beside me.

I didn't even have to look. I felt it. That quiet desperation to be seen. I gave Hunter the head nod: *please distract this clown while I make a break for the car.* I made a beeline for the Porsche and got as far as yanking the seat belt over my torso—but it was too late.

Capello rapped his knuckles on my driver-side window. I rolled it down halfway.

"Something I can do for you, Capello?"

He took his time answering, eyes flicking toward the house, then back to me. "You're a long way from your side of town, Charlie," he said. "What's a guy with your salary doing in a middle-class neighborhood like this?"

I didn't blink. "I go where the cases take me."

He smirked like that was an answer he'd expected. "You got a new partner?"

I glanced at Hunter. "Yeah. Very different from Kane."

Capello nodded. "You ever think about finishing what Kane didn't?"

Damnit. I went still, a second too long.

"You know, Martha Anderson's been calling my office," Capello said. "She says her grandson's case was never properly closed."

I didn't answer.

"Your partner was the lead at the time, correct? Mr. Dawson?"

I adjusted my leather jacket. Capello thought he was leading the conversation, steering me somewhere. I've seen politicians do the same—sidestepping, dodging, thinking they're the smartest in the room. He was fishing. I wasn't biting.

I gave Hunter the nod. She started pulling the address before I even said a word. Capello stayed on the curb, watching us roll out.

Time for a chat with Martha Anderson.

CHAPTER 6

SECRETS CARVED IN SILENCE

NOVEMBER 6TH — 2:05 PM

The wind whispered through the trees at Eagle Head Park, pregnant with the weight of stories left untold. Martha Anderson stood beneath the rotted welcome sign, her cane pressed into the gravel. Her coat flapped against her frame like it barely had anything to cling to.

"You know," she began, her voice cracking under the strain of memory, "the Alderman's been the only one to show up for me. Checked in. Asked if I needed anything." She paused, tears welling. "He's a good man."

I stayed quiet. Hunter glanced my way. The cameras loved the Alderman. So did the headlines.

But I'd seen the truth under his smile—and it always smelled like politics.

Martha sighed. "I'm just his grandmother. He lost his parents. One to drugs, the other to selfishness. And me? I'm just… old."

She looked at us then. Not angry. Just tired. "When you get to be my age, you can't run around with the kids. You can't wrestle or chase them through the woods like you used to. But you also can't keep 'em locked in the house like prisoners. What kind of life is that?" Her voice wavered. "I just didn't have the energy to keep up with him. I wish I had."

She blinked, hard. "That's what cost me. That's what let him slip."

She turned toward the tree line, eyes brimming. "If I had seen anything, and called somebody? Whoever was out there would've had hell to pay. But that's the thing. I didn't see. Because I couldn't. Because this city…" She stopped, swallowed hard. "This city's supposed to help when folks fall behind. But lately, it feels like every service got pulled like a rug out from under us."

She pulled something from her coat. A photograph of a blond-haired little boy—folded at the edges but protected like gold.

She stared at it for a long second, then pressed it to her heart. "I gave Vincent Kane the other one. My second and last photo of Timmy." She offered it to me, arm trembling. "The one I kept. I want you to hold onto it now."

I hesitated. For a moment there, old ghosts beckoned me, from somewhere deep in her watery eyes.

"Please," she whispered. "When you find him—bring *both* home. Him… and the photo. Promise me."

I took it. Gently. The kid's brown eyes smiled up at me, caught forever in a moment before everything broke. "I promise," I said.

She nodded , dried her tears, and faced the path ahead. "I know I don't have anything new to give you. No new information, but I just…had a feeling." She looked down at the ground. "Eagle Head Park has always been his favorite. Maybe, somehow, he'll end up back here."

I grasped her shoulder. "Martha, you head back home now. We'll handle it from here."

Hunter tapped her GPS, activating the location tracking. The blue light flickered against her face. "Signal's good," she murmured.

Martha hesitated. Her mouth tightened like she wanted to say more. But she only exhaled. "Please do call me if you find anything," she said quietly, then turned and disappeared into the night.

I adjusted my coat, jaw locked, and rounded on Hunter.

"Let's move."

The deeper we delved into the woods, the worse it got. Fog wrapped around the trees like a heavy veil. The branches twisted, skeletal fingers clawing at the sky.

And the silence… something was wrong.

Forests have a rhythm. Even at night, you hear movement. Wind shifting. Birds. Whatever. But this?

Dead.

The ground felt soft under my boots, all noise absorbed. The trees loomed closer, and the damp air clung to my skin.

Hunter's voice broke the quiet. "We're on track," she said, the glow of her GPS outlining her chin. "Green trail should break off soon."

I barely registered her. Then—

My boot caught on something. I stumbled forward, flashlight swinging. The beam bounced across the forest floor.

And then I saw it: a tangled mess of decay. I crouched low, my breath tight in my chest. Hunter moved beside me, scanning the ground.

"What the hell is that?" she murmured. The shape was small, but not human.

I pulled a pencil from my coat pocket, careful not to disturb anything. Leaning in, I prodded lightly at the remains, shifting them just enough to see.

No blood. No splatter. Just rot. The ribs curled inward unnaturally, the skull elongated, narrow.

My stomach clenched. "Looks like a dog," I muttered.

Hunter exhaled . "That can't be a coincidence."

No. It couldn't.

I lowered the pencil, eyes scanning for details. The bones were old, stripped clean by time and nature, but something was off.

I pressed my lips together. Was the collar removed? Was the neck broken? I squinted closer, shifting the flashlight…

And that's when I saw it:

Fabric. Half-buried under the decay. I reached in carefully, fingers brushing against something stiff. When I pulled it free, my breath hitched.

It was a child's t-shirt. The color was faded, dirt-stained, but still visible. //Unease crawled up my spine. I started to stand, like gravity had reversed and was pulling me upward.

I *felt* it before I saw it. In the distance, just beyond the trees…

A knife. Jammed deep into the bark, buried up to the hilt. And not just any knife—a military knife.

The sheath was still intact, strapped in like it was waiting for someone to claim it. I took a step forward, my heart pounding.

Something inside me shifted—like I was tilting toward understanding.

I ran. Fast. My tactical boots slid against the leaves, sending me forward on all fours. I tried to push myself up to get my footing, but the damp ground gave way beneath me. I skidded, breath sharp, almost losing balance.

But I didn't stop.

I couldn't.

I reached the tree, hands slamming against the bark on either side of the blade.

My chest heaved, breath rattling out of me. My fingers curled as my eyes locked onto the handle.

There. The compass. Embedded in the grip with its needle trembling. Pointing north.

My vision tunneled. Stamped into the steel was: 37N.

37 North to where? I wondered, my eyes jerking left, right, and center. Before I could stop myself, I reached for the knife, fingers inches from the hilt, when—

I felt Hunter tugging at my jacket. She was pointing to the ground at the base of the tree. A severed dog tag chain, lying atop a scrap of blood-stained fabric. *Familiar.*

Hunter's voice snapped through the fog. "Dawson. What is this?"

I inhaled. The fog thinned just enough to let the air in.

Hunter didn't flinch, her voice dropping to a whisper. "Look at me."

I did.

My stomach flipped. We weren't just in the woods anymore. We were standing in the middle of a damn crime scene.

I pulled my weapon instinctively. "Crime scene! Lock it down! Three hundred feet in every direction!"

Hunter grabbed the radio, jumping into action. "Signal CSI to 37 North. GPS is active. We've got a live one." She looked at the knife. "Potential military case…"

She turned to me, but I was already scanning. Every step we took had walked us straight into a memory I didn't want to remember. She asked the question I didn't dare voice.

"Why did Miss Anderson send us here?"

I couldn't answer even if I wanted to. And that scared the hell out of me.

Hunter lowered the radio, her tone shifting. "How the hell did she know anything was out here?"

"She didn't. Grieving granny, just had a hunch." I shivered. "This wasn't even an active case anymore…"

"No," Hunter said. "This is something else."

"Someone's in my head," I said. "And they're playing for keeps."

Hunter's eyes narrowed.

I turned the radio again. "Rope it off eighty feet in every direction. Nobody touches a damn thing." Hunter relayed the message without hesitation. Professional. And thank God for that, because this? This was no accident. This wasn't random.

This was a *signal*. A bad one. An old military case—buried, sealed, forgotten.

Now unearthed.

I stared at the knife. "I want to know *every single person* she told about this trail."

"And if she's involved?"

"I'm not excluding anyone."

CHAPTER 7

BEHIND THE TAPE

NOVEMBER 6TH – 8:12 PM

F*lash.*

The camera strobes exploded in bursts, bleaching the crime scene white, again and again. The crime scene unit moved in a precise and calculated formation: Evidence bags rustled, tactical boots crushed wet earth, and latex gloves snapped in unison. Floodlights turned the damp leaves into molten gold, and shadows stretched long across the underbrush. They'd taken three hours to reach us this deep in the woods, the last tendrils of daylight long gone from the canopy of trees.

"Move aside."

James's voice was smooth and deliberate. Unrushed, with enough weight behind it to cut through the air. Just like you want from your forensics guy. James exhaled. "Lucky I got here before everyone else. Otherwise, I might've had to implicate you in the crime, seeing as how your tracks are all over it."

I shifted uncomfortably. Hunter did, too.

"*Jesus*," James continued, "we'll have to use a CAD scanner just to tell the evidence from you guys' shoe prints."

I smirked, stepping backward. "Good thing I'm on your good side, then."

James stepped forward like a chess player about to examine the board. He took in the scene the way a surgeon sizes up a body—quick, analytical, cutting.

A knife in a tree. A dead dog. Shredded, bloodied clothes.

He let out a slow breath. "Whoever did this didn't just leave all this out here." His voice was level, but his eyes were sharp. "They're constructing something."

Hunter folded her arms. "They're taunting us?"

James knelt beside the remains, donning gloves. His movements were calm and deliberate, those of a predator assessing its prey. The foul scent of decay permeated the cold air. I could see his jaw tighten beneath his surgical mask.

I knelt beside him as he gently pressed what remained of the flesh with his gloved hand. "Notice how the skin compresses around the neck, indicating there was a collar that's missing." James sighed, stood, and tapped the compass embedded in the knife handle. It flickered but stayed true. "Thirty-seven degrees north." He studied it for a long second before shaking his head. "Not random."

Hunter glanced sidelong at me. "What does it mean?"

I exhaled, rubbing a hand over my jaw. "Could be latitude. It could be a bearing… Either way, it's direction. And direction means planning. Intent."

James's smirk faded. His voice was quieter now. "This isn't an impulse. This is structure."

My stomach tightened. "We're dealing with a Conductor."

Hunter frowned. "A what?"

"A Conductor," I repeated, my voice low. "Someone who doesn't just kill. Someone who orchestrates. Who moves pieces. Who plays the long game."

James exhaled. "He's giving us a trail."

Hunter folded her arms. "A trail to what?"

I turned back toward the tree, the compass, the blade buried deep into the wood…

That was the question. And if I knew one thing about men like this, they didn't leave trails for you to catch them.

They left them to see if you were *worthy*.

I stood up, brushing the dirt off my gloves. James lingered near the scene, eyes fixed on the remains, his mind already working five steps ahead.

Hunter and I ducked under the tape to press further into the woods, the trees swallowing us in shadow.

CHAPTER 8

THE FIRST GLIMPSE OF MADNESS

OCTOBER 31ST – 7:22 PM

The floor creaked first. Then came the smell—dust, old wood, and something burnt.

Then, he noticed it—a faint beep somewhere in the room. Soft. Steady. Off-tempo. Like the house was monitoring something. Then, he saw him.

Tom Caldwell stood in the darkly lit hall, his massive frame filling the doorway to the kitchen, eyes hard and unreadable. He creaked open the door, and for a fleeting moment, he swore the boy seated before him really was the ghost of someone he had lost long ago. The boy—Lucas—trembled, his face as pale as a sheet, feet glued to the floor, pressed against the door like an animal cornered.

"I'm sorry, Mister. Please, don't hurt me…" Lucas's voice cracked, fear rippling through his every word. He looked at Tom, his entire body shaking with what looked like the instinct to flee and the realization that there was nowhere to go.

Tom's heart twisted, and his hand tightened on the doorframe, the weight of what had been and what could never be again weighing down on his shoulders. He managed a gentle smile and extended his hand to draw the boy closer.

"Welcome home, Junior." Tom's rough voice was tinged with enduring sorrow. His hand quivered with compassion and yearning as he reached for Lucas, but the boy flinched away.

"Let me go!" Lucas screamed when the hand found his shoulder, struggling to break free from Tom's grasp.

For an instant, trepidation loosened Tom's fingers, but then he gripped the boy tighter, finding in the move some queer sort of solace. "Junior, listen to me," he whispered quickly. "I've done things—things you couldn't understand—to make it back alive from the war. Your mother. She should've been watching you closer… but she was way too distracted. Especially with everything changing. The world's not what it was—and it's only gotten worse since you've been gone. His voice stumbled, the tightness in his throat worsening.

He saw only panic and confusion plastered across the boy's face. He didn't understand. "Wha-what are you talking about?" Lucas croaked.

Tom paused before responding, basking in the suffocating silence. The kitchen, filled with shadows and mechanical gadgets, felt like it was closing in on them. Lucas averted his gaze, then seemed distracted by the array of unusual devices. He ran his fingers along the wires, observing the odd assortment of items that belonged more in a fortress than a residence.

Still looming behind him, Tom followed the boy's motions with a peculiar feeling of appreciation. The seriousness in his eyes softened for just that moment, though the resoluteness would not vacate them. "Each trap," he continued, "is a safeguard." He jerked his head towards the board that lay before them, with bright nails of steel protruding from it. "They are juniors. They stand guard— protection for you."

Lucas said nothing. He nodded absently, gaze falling to the tripwire running along the floor across the entire room. Perhaps he felt he was stuck in a bad dream. Alas, thought Tom. But to explain everything now would do little to ease the boy's mind. A heavy, uncomfortable silence fell between them, tense enough that a knife could be thrust through it. Tom knew he had better cut it soon.

He cleared his throat, with casualness that did not quite ring true. "Hey, you remember Dad's favorite story?" Tom asked low and almost desperately. "Charles Bronson. You know, the guy who booby-trapped everything and kicked ass?" He chuckled sullenly; warmth had already fled from his tone. "That's where I got the idea for some of these."

Lucas only furrowed his brow. Tom sighed, shaking his head. "Forget it," he muttered, brushing off the attempt at humor, "we'll talk about that later."

Tom's eyes softened, the longer he looked at Lucas. "You're safe now, son." The words came out more like a promise than a statement of fact. "This house is secure. Everything I've accomplished comes from my military training and experience overseas."

Tom reached for a broomstick and wedged it against the radiator, releasing a burst of hot steam that hissed like an angry serpent against the blinds. The pressure sent a gust through the room, pushing both back a step.

"Whooaa!" Tom exclaimed with exaggerated bravado as he crouched down to Lucas's level and placed his hands on the boy's shoulders, his voice softening. "You're safe, you hear me? Safe. We're in this together. Now, general order number one, you must stay away from the windows, Junior. I don't want you ending up like the last person who set off one of these traps."

Lucas stood silent, his legs quivering like jelly. Tom could sense the sheer dread emanating off him; it clung to everything in the room.

As he stood to leave, Tom glanced back from the doorway, his silhouette framed by the dim, flickering light overhead. A ghost of a smile tugged at his lips, a fleeting reminder of some distant, easier time. His voice was now firm, mantra-like, as if he were speaking to himself. "One thing our family of Caldwells knows how to handle is trouble." Tom spat proudly. "Operation Stand Your Ground has commenced. *We defend what's ours.*"

By now, Tom could see he was losing the boy. Lucas's fingers twisted the hem of his shirt over and over, gripping it like a lifeline.

Yet finally, he spoke, his voice small but clear. "Can I ask you something? Do you have a cell phone?"

Tom froze. His eyes sharpened, cutting through the dim light like blades. "What happened to yours?"

Lucas swallowed, shifting to his feet. "I… I left it at home. Jake had his, but he—he left."

Tom's stare didn't break. "Ah. So, you spent all your time running around, pulling pranks, but never thought about keeping a lifeline." He smiled at this foolishness. "Bet you wasted every dollar on toilet paper and fireworks, huh?"

Lucas didn't move, didn't draw a breath.

Tom took a slow step closer. "That's the problem with kids like you. You think it's all a game until it's not… Well, a phone's no good to you now, anyway."

Lucas forced his eyes upward. "Why?"

Tom tilted his head. "Because it's a window. To things you're better off not seeing." He paused, then added, almost to himself, "Predators. The dark web. Have you ever wondered how easy it is for someone to find a kid like you?"

Lucas tensed. "Wh-where's my friend? Oliver. He-he was here too."

Tom exhaled, shaking his head. "Not now, Lucas. No friends. No phones. Not here. Not for a while."

Tom exited the kitchen and closed the door behind him, shutting away the echoing thud of that young, beating heart.

———

84

CHAPTER 9

LINES IN THE SAND

NOVEMBER 1ST – 6:33 PM

Evening light bathed the quiet street in gold, stretching the shadows long and jagged, carving the neighborhood into a patchwork of dark and light. Atop the slight hill across the way, Tom Caldwell was gliding his paintbrush along his porch railings in long, deliberate strokes, clad in a worn flannel and paint-streaked jeans. The scrape, scrape, scrape of bristles against the wood filled out the stillness, a soothing cadence to mask the storms brewing within him and without.

Kordell and his crew swaggered up to his porch with no attempt at stealth. Kordell knew Tom was a military man, knew that—even as he continued to paint—he was surveying them out of the corner of his eye. Fists clenched at his sides, knuckles whitening with the effort of restraint, Kordell leaned against the weather-beaten banister.

He swallowed hard. This wasn't the moment to strike—not yet. He needed to stay in control. His OG had sent him for a reason.

Lil JJ's disappearance, a raw and festering wound, hung over him like a cloud, and now it was time—not for revenge, but for justice.

"What's up, Tom?" Clink's voice sliced through the air, shattering Kordell's train of thought. Tom didn't lift his head or lose the timing of his brush strokes. Impressive, Kordell admitted to himself.

"Evening, peeps," Tom said finally. He rose from kneeling, brush still in hand. His smile was razor-sharp and casual as he opened his arms wide. "Still puffing that K2? Lost in your little fantasy world?" He faked sucking on the brush, letting the mockery hang in the air.

Kordell's heart pounded against his ribs, each taunt feeding the inferno of fury inside him. His lips curled into a snarl as he stepped closer and threw up a gang sign. "I want all the smoke, and you don't want none. Fifth Street and that's on my flag, fool."

Without missing a beat, Tom laughed. "Hey, K! Short on ears, long on mouth." Tom shook his head. "Always yapping, always making promises your little platoon can't keep."

Kordell took another step forward, his temper fraying. "What, do you think I forgot?" he growled, voice low and venomous. "Think I don't remember what you did?"

Tom locked eyes with him, his smirk growing sharper. "Well, you'd better have more than your petty suspicions, or you'll end up wishing you'd never crossed me."

The two men stared each other down, the silence broken only by Clink's sneering laugh.

"You washed-up GI Joe..." Clink spat. "Not only we gonna cross you, Tom. We gonna ex you da fuck *out*." He stepped forward, nearly chest-to-chest with Tom.

Tom didn't flinch. Instead, he tilted his head and spat off to the side, his eyes hard as steel as he shifted his gaze to Clink.

Kordell's hand shot out, grabbing Clink by the shoulder and yanking him backward. His authority was ironclad, teeth grinding as he hissed, "*Fall back, Clink. Now.*"

Clink hesitated but obeyed, stepping back with a grumble. Kordell turned his attention back to Tom, lowering his voice so only the two of them could hear.

"We're not savages," he said, masking the hatred in his voice with calm. "Unless we're forced to be."

Kordell spat onto the ground, and in doing so, noticed a streak of yellow splattered against Tom's chipped siding: raw egg. He'd know that dried residue anywhere, having partaken in his own fair share of mischief on Halloweens past. Suddenly, Kordell grimaced, remembering the pictures of those missing kids on the news. *As if the world weren't hard enough…*

"Not so popular with the neighbor kids, huh?" Kordell laughed, nodding at the dried yolk stains.

Tom's expression didn't change, but a flicker of something dangerous crossed his eyes. He leaned forward , his voice a quiet growl. "That reminds me. Your boy Clink?" he said, changing the subject. "He snatched Mrs. Anderson's purse and blacked her eye. No women, no kids—that's the code. Your platoon is a goddamn joke."

Kordell's composure cracked for just a second as he swallowed his rage once more.

Tom took advantage, shaking his head in mock disappointment. "But how do you guys say it around here?" Tom grinned, his voice almost playful now, brandishing the brush like a weapon. "Say less, right?" He flicked a splatter of paint at their feet. "Enjoy your evening, Kordellious. You're going to need it."

Tom turned his back on Kordell and Clink; grabbed the handle of the old lawnmower leaning against the porch railing. He pushed it toward the backyard, whistling a low, tuneless melody.

Clink whistled. At the gate to the backyard, Tom turned one last time and called out, "You can wait for the right moment all you want. But you better have more than half-baked suspicions when you do. Otherwise, it's your funeral…"

Kordell stood frozen, his chest heaving, his mind swirling in a storm of rage and calculation. Then, he relented, and turned to head back down to the street. Before he took more than a few steps, though, out of the corner of his eye he spotted something glinting in the grass of Tom's lawn. He crept closer and looked down.

It was a lighter, one of those cheap plastic convenience store ones. He pocketed it.

This wasn't the moment, he told himself, signaling to his crew to bounce. But the moment was coming.

And when it did, Tom Caldwell would finally pay for what he'd done.

CHAPTER 10

ENTANGLED IN EVIDENCE

NOVEMBER 7TH – 8:00 AM

The elevator doors slid shut, sealing me in with Hunter, who was holding two cups of coffee. She extended one toward me with a smirk sharp enough to draw blood.

"Morning, Dawson. Two sugars, black. And don't say I never gave you anything."

I raised an eyebrow. "What's the catch?"

"No catch." She shrugged, all smooth confidence. "Yet."

I sniffed the coffee suspiciously. "Should I have forensics check this first?"

Her grin widened. "Relax, Dawson. I don't get rid of partners that easily."

The tiniest dry chuckle escaped me. I took a sip. "Great shooting at the range the other day, Hunter. Though of course, targets don't shoot back."

Hunter's smirk faltered, but she squared her shoulders. "Good thing I don't miss."

She chuckled at that, thankfully. Then nodded at the file in my hand. "What's that?"

"Tom Caldwell." I sighed. "Somebody who never sat right with me." I handed her the papers to inspect while I retrieved my watch from the drawer and donned it. "Military nut job. Cold-blooded. All the newspapers ever did was rave about him and his damn recon unit, how they turned the tide in some bloody fight overseas. A 'war hero', they called him…"

Hunter raised an eyebrow, shuffling through the documents James had pulled for me. "But you disagree?"

"I…" I paused, considering how much to tell this rookie, already too earnest for her own good. One slip, and I'd risk prompting some cheap, automatic 'thank you for your service' from her. Didn't really want to get into an epic discussion of mine and Tom's history now either. "He's got a damn '*BEWARE LANDMINES*' sign nailed to a post in his front yard. Cute, right? Might be the only honest thing about him."

Hunter frowned. "You checked him out yet? Or just waiting for some poor Amazon driver to trip over a claymore?"

"Funny."

I could see she was about to press me further on my crusade against Caldwell,

Patience—one thing I had to learn. When to strike, and when to sit back and let the pieces fall. She was stuck being my partner now, no doubt about that. So maybe it was time I handed her some of the heavier boxes—evidence, observations, the kind of stuff that puts people away.

Time for her science lesson. The elevator descended, the steel walls giving way to reinforced concrete. The glass shaft revealed the sprawling CSI lab below. Hunter's breath caught as the view widened. Holographic displays flickered, weapon prototypes hummed, and touchscreens processed data at speeds that shouldn't have been possible.

"This isn't just a lab," she murmured.

"Nope," I replied. "These guys are pushing the edge of what's possible. " The doors slid open.

The tang of chemicals and latex wafted at us, a scent that stuck in your throat like bad whiskey. James stood at the center of it all, sleeves rolled, gloves tight. He was hunched

over a workbench. Paxton, another forensic tech, leaned against a counter, wearing his signature amused 'I know something you don't' look.

I stepped forward. "James. Is she ready?"

A slow, knowing smile lit James' face. "Not yet," he said. "Still… fine-tuning."

Hunter followed my gaze—then froze at its target, mouth agape. Partially concealed beneath a large sheet lay a sleek and dangerous vehicle. Its contours hinted at an alluring shape, while embedded lasers glimmered subtly across its surface. A single emblem caught the low light—a horse, symbolizing power and elegance.

"Soon," James added. Almost taunting.

I exhaled. "Soon isn't now. Keep at it."

Paxton chuckled from the corner. "Ah, teasing the rookie already, Dawson? Poor Hunter."

"Enough chit-chat, fellas." James cleared his throat . "Feast your eyes on this, detectives," he said, snapping off his gloves like a magician revealing his next trick. He motioned to the military knife lying under the bright white light on the lab table.

I stepped in, crouching slightly. The blade was sharp—but the hilt? That's where the answers were. A glass-covered compass, its needle frozen, was still embedded in the handle. A relic.

"This isn't just some hardware store special," I muttered, running my finger along the worn blade. James grinned. "101st Airborne—Jungle Recon. Rare as hell. Only a few platoons had these."

Hunter leaned in, snapping a picture. "Sending the coordinates and image to Cash and Johnston," she muttered. A second later, her phone buzzed. Sent.

I exhaled, studying the insignia. The Internet wouldn't help; military files weren't on Google, at least not the real ones. "How the hell are we supposed to dig into this?"

James spun the knife under the light. "From what I'm seeing… Platoon Four."

Hunter arched a brow. "So, we think this guy was Army?"

James shrugged. "Could be a Marine. Based on the compass installation, it's a marine unit that requires directional guidance. I'm narrowing it down to a Jungle-trained unit as we speak." James stopped typing, pushed his glasses up, and smirked. "Recruiters must have skipped your mailbox."

"Yeah," Hunter said dryly. "I guess I went straight to fighting crimes instead of perpetrating them."

James tapped the compass. "There's only one coordinate etched on there. But if this is real issue military gear, there's usually a secondary reference. Something to triangulate…"

Hunter leaned over. "So, we're only seeing half the trail."

"Exactly," James said. "It's incomplete by design."

Behind us, Paxton was already crouched over a secondary tray, scanner in hand, slowly working over the lifeless body of the dog, a mid-sized mutt. The thing looked stiff but fresh.

He glanced up, voice flat. "Dog's male. Three years old, give or take. No chip. Stomach's full. Eyes are clear. Dead less than twenty-four hours." He indicated an evidence bag, containing a hoodie sleeve that appeared to be torn by teeth. "This was found ten feet from the body. Kid-sized. Could belong to the boy."

James stepped in. "We're running trace fibers now. But the timing tracks."

Hunter frowned. "What's a dog doing out here with kid clothing?"

James angled his head toward her. "You know what most people miss with dog crime scenes? We follow the paw prints. But the dog… he's tracking things too."

Exactly," I said. "And then there's what it ate. Berries halfway down the trail? That tells us the halfway point. Trash, wrappers, wild meat—each one narrows the location."

James added, "Processed dog food? We can trace the brand against local store orders to narrow it down."

"Which leads us to a supplier," I said. "And eventually, who bought it."

Paxton straightened up. "And just to be clear… dogs eat everything."

"Everything," I repeated.

Paxton gave a half-nod, scanning again. "I would've hoped he was chipped. Had a collar. Makes it easier."

James folded his arms. "Yeah. A collar and no chip? That's like carrying a wallet with no ID.""Maybe they pulled it," I said. "Or maybe someone didn't want him found."

James nodded. "It's not glamorous, but it's evidence. And it holds up in court. Especially when you don't have a body."

I stared at the blade again. The knife was a message. This? The dog, the sleeve, the compass? I took a slow breath. "Start running it. Knife comes first."

Paxton gave a lazy salute. "Roger that, boss."

I turned to James. "Now, could be a long shot, but with missing kids on our hands, can't rule anything out. Run Lucas Bennett first. Look for a pattern."

James pulled up the database and found the case file, squinting at the screen. "Pulled up a preliminary report… no photo yet. Running it now."

I nodded. "Print everything."

James scrolled on, frowning. "This feels… familiar."

Hunter leaned in. "One of yours?"

I exhaled through my nose. "Maybe."

James hesitated. Then he whispered, "Vincent Kane."

Hunter raised an eyebrow. "Kane?"

"Used to be my partner." I did what I could to keep my voice level. "Until he wasn't."

James pulled up an old newspaper clipping. The headline glared back at us: "*Disgraced Agent Vincent Lee Kane Exposed for Evidence Tampering.*"

Hunter read silently. Processing. "He covered tracks? Mixed files?"

"Buried the truth," I said flatly. "A lot of truth."

The overhead fluorescents buzzed like static. The lab was colder than usual—lights low, air stale. James slid the folder across the metal table like it weighed more than it should.

I opened it. No paperclip. No tabs. Photos loose, scattered between fingerprint sheets and empty lab tags. Not standard. Not clean.

Hunter stepped in close behind me, shoulder just brushing mine. She glanced over as I flipped the first page: A single youth sneaker, size 5Y. Torn at the toe. Water-damaged. Mud crusted on the sole.

"This isn't a murder case," I said, eyes still on the photo. "No chalk outlines. No bullet entries. No cause of death."

I flipped the page once more. There, we saw the damaged dog tag, the initials "JJ" carved into the aged steel. I rubbed my face and said, "The FNO kid... this thing initiated a gang. Wars."

Hunter frowned. "A kidnapping triggered all that violence?"

James's voice was grim. "Could be someone's using these gangs as pawns for something bigger."

Paxton whistled softly. "Chess with street soldiers. Bold move."

"Us too, by proxy." I clenched my jaw. "I don't like being anyone's pawn."

"These are called missing evidence files," James explained to Hunter, fingers tapping on the keyboard. "When there's no body, but we find physical items, we catalog them. Normally, they'd sit in a bin collecting dust."

"But not here," I added. "Here, we run them."

Hunter looked between us. "Run them how?"

"DNA matching," James said. "We don't just look for a child's DNA anymore. We cross-reference parental samples. Father and mother profiles help us generate a probable child sequence."

Hunter looked impressed. "That's… ingenious."

"It's the biggest missing persons database in the country," James said. "But it gave too much power to one man."

I closed my eyes. "Vincent Kane." Hunter's posture shifted.

James went on. "Kane… had unrestricted access. Started pulling files, connecting patterns before the rest of us even saw the data." Hunter started to ask a question, but I closed the folder, cutting her off.

"That's enough on Kane," I said. Silence shrouded our corner of the lab.

Paxton finally cut through it with his usual brand of offbeat timing. "Well, if we're done ghost-hunting… someone want to tell her why Dawson's still vertical?"

Hunter blinked. "Huh?"

James smirked. "The defibrillator."

I made a show of rifling through the case file again, but I could feel all their eyes on me.

Hunter tilted her head. "You wear a defibrillator?"

"Something Paxton cooked up," James answered. "Didn't want to see the old dog go out early."

Hunter studied me, like she was looking for my old smirk, or any flicker of emotion. "How long have you worn it?"

I didn't answer.

James jumped in. "It kicks in when his body forgets it's alive."

Paxton grinned. "Automatic Rhythm Pulse Defibrillator. ARPD. Built it myself. Tiny charge. Just enough to remind his heart not to clock out when he forgets to sleep."

"But… why?" Hunter whispered. "What hap–?"

I slapped the folder shut again and turned toward the computer screen. "Let's stay on the kid. Jerald Jenkins. Keep digging."

With that, the room shifted. Hunter gathered the remainder of the files; held them tightly in her arms.

Then her phone buzzed. She scanned it and stiffened. "Jake Smith's parents found a transit pass tucked deep in the seam of his jeans. Hill Section line. Not even stamped."

James blinked. "So, he moved. That puts him out of any last known location."

"Exactly," Hunter said. "We've been looking in the wrong damn place."

James let out a breath, then swiped open a digital map. "Hill Section's massive. We'll need to break it down into quadrants."

"We already are," I said. "Lower Big East, start there."

Hunter tapped her tablet. "All right. Reset the grid. Prioritize Hill Section Quadrants. Pull transit footage, facial recognition— whatever isn't scrubbed."

Paxton grinned. "This gets better and better."

James pulled up a new feed. "One more issue. Mischief Night."

Hunter narrowed her eyes. "What about it?"

James tapped the screen. "Hundreds of kids in black hoodies, masks, all running around that night. If our guy moved Jake, then what? He disappeared in the noise."

My jaw clenched. "Perfect."

James glanced at me. "All AI footage has to be manually reviewed now. It's slow."

I grabbed my coat. "Then start early. James; hit the Hill Section transit feeds. Paxton, start filtering Mischief Night footage by unusual patterns."

Hunter looked at me. "Where are we going?"

I adjusted my collar. "Someplace that doesn't delete the truth."

CHAPTER 11

THE MILL OF CLUES

NOVEMBER 7TH – 9:35 AM

The rain fell in sheets, turning the city into a blur of neon reflections and wet asphalt. The Porsche's wipers struggled against the downpour. I gripped the wheel, navigating the slick roads.

Hunter sat silent beside me, arms crossed. Eventually, she spoke. "So, we're skipping protocol to visit a newspaper mill?"

She exhaled, watching the city pass in a haze of streetlights and fractured shadows. I could tell she was thinking—piecing things together on her own, but still, waiting for me to explain.

I wouldn't. Some things you have to see for yourself.

Ahead, the Big East Independent Tribune loomed through the rain—an old, weatherworn structure, its brick exterior streaked with grime and faded murals from another era. The last of its kind.

I pulled up to the curb, tires splashing through a shallow puddle.

After climbing out of the car, Hunter hesitated, glancing at the flickering sign above the door. "This place doesn't look like it's seen business in a decade."

I winked. "That's the idea." I knocked twice on the steel door.

Silence. Then, a small panel slid open, revealing sharp, dark eyes. "Yes?"

"We're here for Danielle," I said, water cascading from my collar.

A pause. Then the door creaked open, revealing a man with ink-stained fingers and bulky earmuffs around his neck. The sharp, chemical smell of ink and damp paper hit me instantly, stinging my eyeballs.

"You're expected," the man said, stepping aside. Hunter hesitated a half-second before following me inside.

"Welcome to the Vault."

The first thing you noticed was the sound. Not the usual city noise, but the steady rhythm of printing presses. The metallic clank and churn of machines, paper feeding through rollers, ink spilling into stories. Stacks of bundled newspapers lined the walls. Filing cabinets stood tall, their drawers locked. Typewriters clacked somewhere in a distant corner.

Hunter's eyes flicked around, taking in the frenetic surroundings. She ran a hand along a nearby desk, her fingers picking up traces of dust and old ink. Her brow furrowed. "What kind of paper mill needs this much secrecy?"

I didn't answer. She wasn't ready for it yet.

We moved through the space, past rows of aging machinery, past workers hunched over papers, their hands stained black with ink.

They weren't just printing news.

They were archiving it.

Hunter's fingers brushed a yellowed headline from years ago: Political scandal. Murder investigation. A missing kid.

At the back of the factory, away from the machines, a heavy metal door led to a smaller, dimly lit office. The air inside felt denser and more oppressive, filled with the aromas of aged books, ink, and cigarette smoke.

Danielle Marcella sat behind a cluttered desk, a Chesterfield dangling between two fingers. She stubbed it out as we stepped inside, barely glancing up. "Dawson," she muttered, voice rough as sandpaper. "I could feel you coming from a mile away." She paused. "And, judging by the sound of heels clicking on the floor, you brought company."

I rolled my eyes. "Good to see you too, Danielle."

She finally looked up, eyes locking on Hunter, who squared her shoulders. Danielle studied her for a moment, then exhaled a puff of smoke. "Ah, the new partner."

"Detective Emily Hunter."

I slid a folder from my coat and placed it on the desk. "Show her the pictures."

Hunter hesitated before laying out crime scene photos and evidence shots. The pieces of the puzzle.

Danielle flipped through them. On the third photo, she stopped. Held it a second too long, fingers tapping lightly against the desk.

Hunter noticed. Her eyes flicked to me. Why aren't you pushing her? they seemed to ask.

Because this isn't an interrogation, I would tell her. Save your battles.

Danielle stood, moving toward a massive filing cabinet. She pulled out a thick folder and tossed it onto the desk. I flipped it open.

Written inside were detailed specs on the knife: the SaberTech M9 Tactical. Military issue. Discontinued years ago.

Hunter frowned. "Why pull it?"

"SaberTech partnered with Emtek on a special design," Danielle said, through another cloud of smoke. "New alloy. Built-in compass. The project failed."

Hunter's breath caught. She looked at the photo of our evidence.

Danielle nodded. "Only one platoon had access to the Emtek variant."

Hunter glanced at me. "That's our confirmation."

I nodded slowly. "It's them."

The room stilled. This wasn't just a weapon.

This was a signature.

Danielle kept speaking about the project specs, but my eyes were on Hunter. I could see it—her wheels turning. This girl was sharp. She'd been skeptical when we pulled up, but now? Now she was starting to get it.

This wasn't just a paper mill. This was a vault. A community-run CSI.

The archives didn't just hold headlines—they held evidence. Clues. Patterns. Tips gathered from people who didn't trust the system but trusted this place.

Danielle slid open another drawer, this one full of case files, newspaper and magazine clippings, P.I. reports. She looked up. "You can scrub anything off digital. One click, and it's gone forever. But paper? Paper remembers."

I glanced at Hunter again. Her posture had changed. She finally understood why we were here.

Why Danielle mattered.

Why this place mattered.

Danielle let the drawer slam shut, the echo punching through the room. She took a slow drag from her cigarette, exhaled through her nose. Smoke curled across the light.

"They want to shut us down," she said flatly. "In the age of social media news, we're the last defense of objectivism." Danielle smiled. "But here? Our records are never compromised. As long as we keep an eye on who we hire as editors, anyway." Then she turned to Hunter, eyes sharp. "And if I have to spell out who's involved in *that war*?" She leaned in, voice dry and loaded.

"Then you might as well hand me your badge, darling."

Danielle opened one last filing cabinet, pulled up another stack of articles, and slid a newspaper clipping across the desk. An old headline: "*Commander Aspen Leads Jungle Recon to Decisive Victory.*"

I gazed at the grainy image of Aspen and his team—Jungle Recon, four soldiers, their faces obscured by dust and conflict.

Hunter squinted at the photo. "Aspen? You heard of him?" She started searching on her phone, tapping the screen furiously. Ten seconds later, she muttered, "Got something."

I stepped closer, glancing at her phone. It was a private social media profile with the username: *Cage, Jungle Recon.*

I exhaled. "Not exactly subtle."

Hunter scrolled on through his posts, photos… The guy certainly wasn't hiding, a former soldier without a mission—and now, without a leash.

That made him dangerous. Reckless.

"I thought these guys were covert," Hunter said. She showed me an old military photo, him with his platoon, probably. And then I saw it.

"*Caldwell?*" I gasped, grabbing the phone from her. There was no mistaking that face. "This guy was in Tom Caldwell's unit."

Hunter's brow jumped. "That guy you're tracking? What's he got to do with this?"

I shook my head. "We are going to damn well find out. Cage is a person of interest now." I leaned back, thinking. "We need to pull threads. Any last known address?"

Hunter shook her head. "Not yet."

I nodded toward her phone. "Send it to Cash."

Cash had been on the beat for seven years, walking the streets of the Big East. Long before he was a detective, he learned the city from the ground up—not from reports, not from surveillance, but from the people.

If anybody could interpret the whispers of the streets, it was Cash.

Hunter hit send on her message. It was something. A trail. A lead. Moments later—three dots, typing. Then Cash's reply: *I'm on it.*

I sighed, grabbing my coat, adjusting the badge clipped to my belt. "Now we wait."

"Well, Detectives," rasped Danielle, as if her day were full of brusque encounters like this. "It's been a pleasure."

For a moment—barely a blink—Danielle looked like she was about to tell me something. Her eyes glazed over, as if waging an internal battle. Then, her armor was back up. "If anyone can do it, Detective… It's the guy crazy enough to think this district still believes in truth."

She said it like a curse wrapped in a compliment—and meant both.

As Hunter and I left the mill, she turned to me. "This *isn't* just a newspaper mill."

I smiled, donning my shades against the morning rays. "Took you long enough."

CHAPTER 12

LATE NIGHTS AND COFFEE RUNS

NOVEMBER 8TH – 8:40 PM

I usually don't start my day with a hit of caffeine, like most people do. The ones who want to keep sharp, keep moving. Keep burning through textbooks or bad decisions straight through the night. They're prolonging their day, at whatever cost.

Me? I drink coffee to end mine. To cut through the static and settle the weight of the day. Keep my head clear after the city has tried to dull it.

This café did the trick. It was the kind of place where, when you walked in, the world slowed down just enough so you could breathe. Soft conversation, the hiss of steam from the espresso machine. I ordered, then leaned against the counter, eyes drifting over the room.

Kelsey Rose.

She stood at the other end of the counter, hair loose, wearing jeans and a simple top. No mic, no notebook—just her. The way you never see reporters.

I grinned, sidling over to her. "Funny seeing you here, Ms. Rose. No camera to shove in my face?"

She looked up, startled, before amusement flickered through her expression. "Detective," she said, "I never expected to see you so… off-duty."

I inclined my head , matching her energy. "Even detectives get a break." I nodded at the barista. "How about I buy you a drink?"

She raised an eyebrow, something wry curling at the corner of her lips. "I don't mix work with pleasure, Detective."

I chuckled; voice dropping just enough. "Who said anything about work?"

She held my stare for a beat, then exhaled, shaking her head. "Dawson, I know more about you than you think. You work hard, sure. But that doesn't make you perfect."

She threw the words with such ease–teasing, dismissive, unreadable. I didn't have a comeback.

She smiled again. Then, before I could think too much about it, she reached into her bag, pulled out a pen, and wrote her number on the back of a napkin.

Old school. No fuss. Fantastic.

She slid it across the counter with a flick of her wrist.

I picked up the napkin, turning it between my fingers, the red ink still fresh.

When I looked up again, she was gone.

No drinks, huh?

We'll see.

CHAPTER 13

ROOKIE NIGHTMARES

NOVEMBER 9TH – 6:07 AM

The grey light of dawn bled through the squad car windows back at headquarters. The city was waking up. Me, though? I never went to sleep. Cases like this didn't let you.

Kids, just *gone*. The streets were slipping. I'd seen plenty of crime waves come and go, but this? This was something else. I exhaled, rubbing my hand over my jaw. Might as well get this over with.

"All right," I muttered at Hunter. "Long day ahead, so let's get something straight. If we're going to be seeing this case through together, tell me—who the hell am I trusting to cover my ass?"

She straightened. "I graduated top of my class at the academy. Worked patrol for a few years. Helped take down a human trafficking ring last year."

I grunted. "Not bad." I already knew all that, of course, but paper trails often didn't mean shit in the field. "Still don't see why the Chief stuck you with me."

She tilted her head . "Maybe he thought you could learn a thing or two."

"Oh, so you got jokes?"

She shrugged. "Figure if I'm stuck with you, I might as well entertain myself."

I let out a dry chuckle. Not bad. Not bad at all. I cranked the ignition and pulled out onto the road.

Rookies. They're always around, but usually easy to avoid day to day. Women, though? They knew how to pick apart details, how to get under your skin, dig things out you didn't even realize were there.

Hunter had that knack, but she had something else, too: balance. At least there was that to be thankful for.

A silence passed between us. The city rolled by, neon signs flickering out as the sun took over.

"So, Dawson, what's your story?" she finally asked.

I have a low laugh—the kind that betrayed the years behind it. "Let's see. Been on the force nearly twenty-five years. I started in patrol and worked my way up. I've seen it all—drugs, murders, gang wars. The good, the bad, the downright stupid."

She nodded. "Twenty-five years is a long time."

"It ain't a career, it's a sentence."

She smirked. "So why not retire?"

I glanced at her sideways. "Because the city's too damn messy."

She let that sit. Smart move.

I tapped the steering wheel. "Along the way, you learn things. Like how to spot a liar. Colleagues call me 'the human lie detector.' If I have one piece of advice for you, it's this: Trust your gut. People give themselves away if you pay attention. Might keep you alive."

She nodded. I almost smiled. Then—

"What about Kane?"

I clenched my teeth. *Rookies.* "Not today, Hunter."

We turned onto a quieter street, en route toward the day's first crime scene. The city outside was still wrapped in shadows, but the case? It was getting clearer by the second.

After a while, I spoke again, my voice softer. "Grew up here. In the projects."

She looked at me, surprised.

"My grandma and I used to share a bed," I continued. "Used to duck behind the cast-iron radiator when the crack epidemic hit. Now? It's Zoom. They took an old Commodore music hit and named a drug after it."

She let the words settle. Zoom wasn't just another dime bag special. Back in the day, you smoked a little pot, or maybe, if you were feeling adventurous, you hit some peyote—went looking for God and found yourself in a 7-Eleven parking lot instead. Now? Now, they mixed chemistry and chaos and called it progress.

Hunter got a call. "It's Jake's parents, one of the missing kids."

I leaned in. "What'd they say?"

She listened a minute longer, then hung up. "Apparently, he came home. Just for a second. Didn't say much, grabbed something from his room, and left again in a hurry."

That wasn't right. "Did they check his room?" I asked.

"They did, yeah, after he left," she said. "Nothing weird, except his jeans had dried egg on them, inside a pocket.

"So… that thing Paxton gave you."

I sipped my coffee. "Automatic rhythm pulse defibrillator."

She frowned. "And you've needed it… How many times?"

I gave her a sidelong glance. "One restart this past year."

Her expression shifted—calculating. "One restart too many?"

I smirked. "Depends who you ask."

I turned off at the next exit, changing direction. "Time for a detour. Call Johnston and Cash and get them en route."

The courthouse pulsed with constant urgency—lawyers weaving through corridors, clerks hurrying to and from desks, the steady click of dress shoes on polished floors. Everything here had a rhythm— except us. We weren't here to keep the flow moving.

We were here to disrupt it.

At our clerk's desk, Cash leaned in first, tapping his fingers against the cheap wood veneer. "Excuse me miss, but we need this warrant signed *today.*"

The clerk barely glanced up, flicking through a different stack of papers. "Gotta be signed by Judge Helmsley…"

Johnston sighed, squinting at the courthouse clock. "Then we'll come back tomorrow."

I snapped my head toward him. "No. We handle it today."

Hunter leaned over the desk and speed-read the clerk's calendar. "According to this, Helmsley had a 10:30 appointment." She tapped her watch: 10:33. "He should be passing through any second."

Then, right on cue, Judge Alex Helmsley appeared at the far end of the hallway, robe draped over his shoulder, a legal folder tucked under his arm. His stride was quick, eyes locked on his watch.

I stepped into his path. "*Allllex.*"

Helmsley barely slowed. "Charlie. What do you want?"

I clapped twice. "What do I want? Oh, nothing much. Just to introduce you to the fine men and women you employ." I gestured toward my team with mock enthusiasm. "Meet Cash, Johnston, and Hunter. Your guys."

He exhaled, rubbing his temple. "You're really screwing up my schedule, Charlie."

I shrugged. "And I meditate for stress relief, Alex."

Helmsley's gaze flicked toward Hunter. "What is this about?"

She flipped through her notepad. "We need a warrant for Private Bradley Cage. Surveillance confirms he's been purchasing Zoom in the South Side sector." She flipped the pad shut and met his eyes. "Detective Cash's informant confirmed it. Johnston here corroborated the source."

Helmsley shifted the folder under his arm. "Cage is military."

Johnston nodded. "Yes, sir."

"Military hero turned drug addict," Helmsley pondered. "Sounds less than promising." He opened the folder Johnston offered and flipped through the documents. His tone shifted slightly. "Zoom's been seeping in from the next sector for months. I don't like it."

I kept my voice level. "He's been at large for two years. What do you say? Let's get Cage off the streets."

Something turned behind his eyes—a hesitation. Then, after a bit of grumbling—maybe just to get me out of his hair—he signed the warrant.

"There," I said, watching the slow progress of Helmsley's loopy signature. "Almost feels like the law is starting to be the law again."

Cash and Johnston took the warrant, already moving toward the clerk's office to make it official.

Helmsley gave me a slight nod—a silent question: *Is it clear to talk business in front of Hunter?*

I didn't blink. "She's solid. We're the law, remember?"

Helmsley exhaled through his nose, shifting his weight. "Well, you know how it is. A little policy here, a little policy there. Sometimes, you gotta do a favor to get a favor."

I tilted my head. "I don't do favors. I do what's right for the community."

His face scrunched, either amusement or irritation. "That's not how the world works, Charlie."

I stepped in closer and lowered my voice two octaves. 'Maybe not your world.'

Helmsley's smirk barely held. "You act like we're on opposite sides."

I laughed. "We are. You write the laws. We shovel the shit in the streets to enforce them." I leaned in a fraction further. "So don't mistake me for a politician, Alex. I'm not here to play."

Helmsley studied me for a beat. Then, with a slow nod, he adjusted his robe over his shoulder. "I'll remember that."

"See that you do." I pulled another file from my coat and handed it over. "This too."

Helmsley sighed. "You always have something."

I tapped the folder. "Tom Caldwell."

Not the kind of twitch you get when someone says your name. No—this was trained silence. Controlled. Studied.

There was a glint behind the stillness. I took a mental note. The room didn't get quieter—but my mind did.

"Do you have evidence of a crime?" he asked, tone flat as a heart monitor. Unreadable.

I winked. "Working on it."

His fingers hovered over the folder for a beat—just long enough for me to clock it—before he tucked it under his arm like a trophy.

"I'll get to it when I can," he said.

That was it.

Across the hall, Johnston and Cash emerged, holding up the signed warrant like a trophy.

"All wrapped up."

"One step closer."

Hunter glanced at me. "Hey, look—the system worked."

I sighed, jaw tightening. "Sure, you go ahead and think that."

CHAPTER 14

OPERATION GREEN LIGHT

NOVEMBER 9TH – 5:09 PM

I scanned the conference room of the precinct and addressed my scrambling team, my voice razor-sharp. "Listen up." Silence fell. "We got a location."

Johnston leaned forward. "Where?"

Cash tapped the board. "The Ville—New Hall Ville. Right outside Big East Hill Section 17."

I nodded. "Thanks to Cash, we finally got a shot at this. Now, we need Cage alive. Every one of you that brings someone in *breathing*—lunch is on me."

Johnston smirked. "Lunch? That's it?"

I tilted my head. "Lunch might not mean much to you, but it means a hell of a lot to Cash."

The room erupted in titters. Cash folded his arms, shaking his head. "Man, screw you, Dawson."

I went on. "No pistols. No sidearms. We're going full tactical. Rifles, shields, non-lethal rounds unless necessary." My face turned grim. "This is a populated area. We move in stealth. We hit hard, hit fast, and get out."

Just then, the door swung open. Chief Avery barreled in, his sharp eyes locking onto mine almost immediately. I made a beeline for him.

"Dawson, what do you want?"

I grinned. "Oh, nothing, Chief. Just that truck I've been asking for. You know, the one you never gave us."

Chief Avery sighed, rubbing his forehead. "You got a lead?"

I nodded. "A strong one. And I need that truck to move fast."

The Chief folded his arms. "Take the battering ram from 4B."

I shook my head. "No, Chief. We need 4A."

His stare hardened. "And what makes you think you deserve 4A?"

I didn't blink. "Because you want these guys to learn, right? You want them to be safe? That truck is a safeguard. If we roll in with anything less, I can't guarantee we all walk out."

The Chief sighed again, then reached into his pocket, pulled out the inventory keys, and tossed them at me.

I caught them and turned towards the exit.

Avery called after me, "You put even one scratch on it—"

I cut in, "I'll treat it like my very own."

The Chief scoffed. "That's exactly what I'm afraid of." He stalked toward his office, then paused at the doorway, throwing one last look over his shoulder. "Dawson, I'm on your ass like back pockets. Don't forget that."

I twirled the keys in my palm. "Wouldn't dream of it, Chief."

I turned back to the team. "Alright, boys and girls. Gear up. We ride in thirty."

The real test was about to begin.

At 0600 hours, we rolled into the grim streets of The Ville in the 4A truck, a beast built for war—iron-plated, barred windows. A fortress on wheels. I gripped the steering wheel tight, eyes locked ahead, scanning the road.

"Alright," I murmured, slowing to a crawl. "Anybody want to get out, get out now."

Johnston smirked. "Ain't no respawn button. No resets. This is the real deal."

I nodded. "Good. Keep your eyes up, triggers tight. We're cops, not killers. But we will come home tonight."

I inched the truck forward, then stopped one house down—a strategic retreat point.

I set my untouched coffee on the dashboard, still hot. That bitter heat was nothing compared to what was coming.

In the back room, Bradley Cage was busy tying a bandana around his arm, preparing to inject a fresh dose of Zoom. He was jittery, hands twitching in anticipation of the burning sweet hit. The glow-in-the-dark liquid shimmered in the syringe like a lava lamp, inches from his skin.

His crony, Brutus, sat on the couch, a half-conscious mess, while infomercials droned on the television. The room itself reeked of burnt chemicals and sweat.

Outside, shadows moved against the dim streetlights. Somewhere in the distance, a pit bull barked.

A pair of early morning joggers turned their heads toward a rustling sound—the crunch of leaves under heavy boots—then gasped.

A line of police officers in full tactical gear moved through the neighborhood. The leader at the front put his finger on his lips, then waved a signal: *fall back.*

The joggers turned and retreated. Other people, disappeared behind locked doors, some lingering to peek through their blinds. They'd seen raids before.

And they knew how ugly they could get.

6:06 AM

We moved like quiet lightning behind the fence, in near darkness. I fell back, watching my team take position.

And then, Johnston—of all people—took point.

First up. Silent signal. *Hold.*

He pointed to his eyes: keep watch. Pointed to his mouth: Stay quiet. Leading the charge. I was impressed.

Until I saw it—a small, blinking green light above the door. A camera, augmented, motion-triggered.

Just like that, we were already made.

Shit.

Cage froze. He was seconds from sweet relief, the needle hovering over his eager, pulsating vein. Was it paranoia? Maybe. But he knew to trust those senses when they came.

He glanced at his laptop on the end table. Brushed the touchpad to wake the screen—the motion brought the security interface online.

A split-second delay.

Facial recognition blinked red.

A heat signature map pulsed in the corner.

There was only one thing that could have made him drop that needle.

He stood. "Brutus. *Brutus*! We're not alone."

I gritted my teeth. "They know we're here." I mimed to Hunter to go circle around the back of the house, and she crept off.

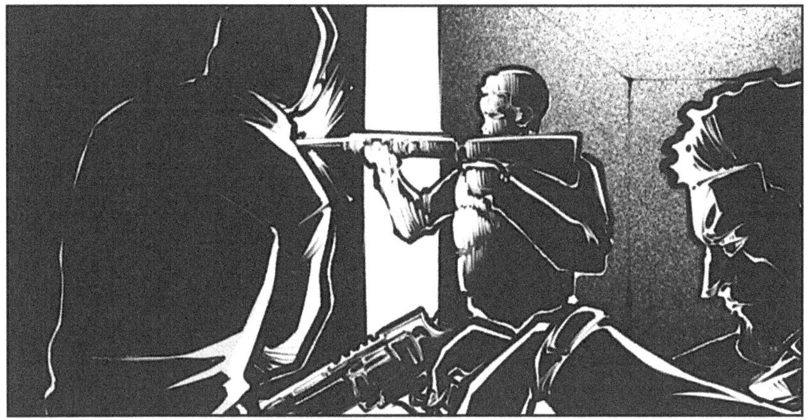

Cash's posture changed. His usual smooth confidence? Gone. He cocked his rifle back.

BOOM.

The damn doorknob blew clean off.

Then—BANG. In one swoop, Cash kicked the door in, so hard the hinges cracked.

I blinked. Didn't know Cash had that in him, big guy, bipolar as hell.

I was starting to like him.

Before the door even hit the ground—

BRRRRRRRRATATATATATATAT. Private Cage opened fire.

Bullets ripped through the air. Wood splintered. Glass shattered. Sparks rained from a busted light.

"TAKE COVER!" Johnston dove behind a broken armchair. Cash slid behind a coffee table.

I hit the floor just as a bullet sliced through my sleeve. God, don't let me die in this shithole. I backed up against the wall, figured I could maybe let the rookies run the show for a bit.

About the worst decision I could've made.

Cage was cackling wildly, firing blind. "OINK, OINK, PIGGIES! COME GET ME!"

Johnston and Cash were so locked onto him, they were neglecting to check whether any other threats might be lurking in the house. While the rookies moved in, I counted. One mag. Thirty rounds.

It was almost music, the rhythm, the breaks. Then—

Silence.

I smirked. "You done?"

Cage snarled, slapping in another mag. *Click. Click.* "PLENTY MORE!" His voice shook the walls. He let loose another wave of projectile thunder. I counted.

Johnston joined me at the wall, panting . "We're pinned."

I inhaled slowly. Military-issue. 5.56 caliber. Standard rifle loadout. I knew the count. Twenty-eight, Twenty-nine, thirty. "Now, he's out again."

Suddenly, Cage popped up from behind the sofa, gun ready to blaze.

Click. Empty.

I smirked. "Told you."

Suddenly, Johnston launched over the chair like a linebacker and slammed into him, They hit the ground, rolling.

I stood back, I thought I'd give them the floor.

Almost the worst damn decision I could've made.

They were so locked on Cage, they forgot about the real monster lurking in the back. Brutus. I readjusted my aim—just in case. You don't survive as long as I have by trusting junkie warheads and half-cleared corners.

Cage was screaming nonsense, trying to slam another mag into his rifle—now both were scrapping for Johnston's assault rifle like it was the last ticket out of hell.

I took a step forward. Cash was already moving.

But fate had jokes.

Cash's boot caught a loose lamp cord— wrapped around his ankle. The lamp yanked off the nightstand and crashed down next to him. Cash grunted, flattened, reaching for anything.

The only thing he could grab? Cage's leg.

So, he bit down.

Cage howled. "BRUTUS!"

And just like that, the floor shook.

Brutus exploded into the room—a dreadlocked slab of muscle, eyes twitching,. Shirtless, barefoot, high as sin. He charged straight toward Johnston, gun raised, teeth bared like some back-alley berserker.

I leveled my 357. The steel rested against the top of my wrist. No shake. No mercy.

"This ain't gonna be clean " I muttered,

This round, was going to send him back to whatever junky god he came from.

Then—

BZZZZZZZZZT.

A jolt of electricity cracked through the air. Brutus convulsed, sending stray bullets into the ceiling. As plaster rained overhead; knees folding like scaffolding. Smoke curled from his shoulders

I lowered the Magnum, whistling low. "Damn. I'd take a slug over that any day."

Hunter stood behind him, taser still live in her hand, eyes locked, stone-cold.

Cash let out a slow breath, adjusting his vest. He toed the lamp that had bested him. "Damn. Looks vintage."

I stared at Brutus's crumpled body. Jaw clenched. Hunter stared at me while Cash and Johnston moved to hold Cage down—two against one.

Hunter exhaled, then smirked. "Hey boys, someone hungry?" She indicated the nasty bite mark on Cage's leg.

Cash coughed. "Tactical disadvantage."

This kid's an animal. I crossed my arms over the defib at my sternum; the chrome plate was dripping with sweat. "Tactical my ass—you bit him."

Johnston pushed Cage to a kneeling position on the floor and zip-tied his wrists behind his back. Cage's chest rose and fell, like that of a roped-up animal.

I gave Johnston the order. "Rip his shirt open." Johnston stepped on Cage's leg and tore the shirt clean off.

There it was. A skull, mouth clenched shut in eternal silence; one skeletal hand clutching a bow and arrow, the other gripping a block of C4. The Covenant Jungle Recon. The truth, staring us dead in our faces.

A soldier's mark. But not just any soldier.

Something beyond the military.

Something buried in history—until now.

Cage sneered, eyes burning with something deeper and more frightening than defiance.

I couldn't banish the feeling that we'd just kicked the hornet's nestI leaned closer, eyes tracing the ink like a war map. "That ain't a tattoo," I said….."That's a warning label."

CHAPTER 15

THE DENIED FILES

NOVEMBER 10TH – 11:30 AM

What the hell is going on with these rookies? I watched from behind the two-way mirror, arms crossed, rubbing my jaw. Johnston and Cash were already screwing this up. They'd been to the academy, sure. Guess they needed some real-life experience, though.

Inside the interrogation room, Cage looked way too comfortable. He let my team burn themselves out while he leaned back, sneering through his withdrawal. I sighed.

Alright, time to step in.

Johnston slammed his hands on the table. "Let's start off with who's selling this Zoom, then we'll talk about your buddy Tom Caldwell."

Cage's expression soured. "Tom Caldwell?" He spat the name out like it burned his mouth. "You don't know shit."

Johnston and Cash exchanged a glance. "What are you talkin' about?" Cash said, his brow furrowing.

Cage let out a dry, bitter laugh. "I'm more afraid of *him* than of you." He leaned back in his chair. "He's a war devil."

Cash scoffed. "How about you give yourself more credit?"

Cage's laugh turned maniacal. "I broke the oath of the brotherhood. I started using guns. In recon? That's a no-go." He exhaled , eyes flitting to the ceiling. "Sorry, detectives. I got no incentive to talk. My days are already numbered."

Johnston's fists clenched. "Talk, and you'll have the cops' protection."

Cage snorted. "From Caldwell?" His voice dropped, laced with something close to horror. He shook his head. "You're in over your head. I'd rather be exed out by real men than rot in your toy cop custody."

Johnston slammed his fist on the table again. "Tell me!"

Cage didn't flinch. Just leaned back, cocky. "Rather rot here."

"Damn it, Cage! Can't you see what we are—"

"*Enough.*" My voice cut through the air like a blade. I stepped inside, Hunter at my heels.

Playtime's over.

Johnston looked like he wanted to argue. But one look at my face, and he knew. I gave them a nod toward the door. "Out. Now."

Cash shot Cage one last glare, muttering under his breath, before storming out. The door clicked shut.

And then it was just me, Hunter, and Cage. I turned to Hunter, dropping my voice low. "Alright. I'm the nice cop."

She raised an eyebrow. "And that makes me…?"

"Worse." I grimaced. "They just tried bad cop. We're about to play better cop."

Hunter exhaled. "Got it."

I pulled out a chair and sat down slow. "Private Cage," I began, my voice calm, steady. "Let's have a conversation."

He sneered. "Is that what we're doing? Felt more like a dick-measuring contest earlier."

I smiled. "Yeah, well, Johnston's new. He's still figuring out how to handle guys like you. You don't break 'em by barking—you break 'em by letting them bury themselves."

Cage huffed, shaking his head. "You think you know me, huh?"

Hunter leaned in, arms folded. "We know enough."

"Doubt it," Cage scoffed, shifting in his chair, cuffs rattling.

I sighed, rubbing my jaw. "Alright, let's speed this up. We already got your connection to Caldwell. We're working on Bronson—Tom's pal. And now we're coming for you." I pushed a photo across the table.

Cage's eyes flickered downward. The picture was clear: four men. Cage, Tom Caldwell, Bronson, and one more. A man only known, according to the file sent over to us, as Snake.

I scrutinized Cage's wavering expression. "Yeah, we're going to pay your boy Tom a visit and tell him everything you told us." I risked a bluff. "About the knife."

Cage snapped his head up. "I haven't told you shit."

I smiled. "Not yet."

He leaned forward, gritting his teeth. "Tom kept us alive."

"Oh yeah, I heard about that," I scoffed. "And what happened when he got back?"

Silence. Then, Cage's jaw tensed. "We… were at war. He lost his son." His voice dipped, almost like he was talking to himself. "Fought for years. Lost his guys over there, and when he came home, he lost it and his son, too." Cage shivered, from memory, withdrawal, or both. "Man comes back to nothing. How do you think that messes with a soldier?"

Hunter spoke first. "Enough to turn him into a monster?"

Cage let out a dry laugh. "Monster? Maybe. But he's the only reason any of us made it back. I'd never betray him. Not after what he did for us."

I nodded . "Loyalty's a hell of a drug." Cage grunted. I tilted my head. "Speaking of drugs—you want Zoom? I got two options: jail or rehab."

His lip curled. "Do you have drugs in jail?"

"Sure." I shrugged. "The difference is, one keeps you standing, and the other makes sure you leave in a box."

His eyes darkened. "I don't have a problem."

Hunter scoffed. "Yeah? Those needle marks in your arm say different."

Cage only stared at me, breathing heavy. Then I saw it.

That flicker of doubt.

The slow realization.

I sat back, grinning. "We're not here to save you, Cage. We're here to take down everyone left in your platoon. Caldwell. Bronson. Maybe even Aspen. Unless, of course, the rest of them had nothing to do with it." I leaned forward again, enjoying the twitch of Cage's jaw.

Cage swallowed. Hard. His gaze dropped to the picture again. "Bronson…" His voice was barely above a whisper.

"He's still active?" Hunter asked.

Cage nodded. "Yeah."

I exhaled. "And Snake?"

Cage's lips parted, but he shook his head. "Don't know much about Snake. But Bronson?" He exhaled sharply. "Yeah. He's still out there."

I leaned back, satisfied. Now we had something to go on. I stood, adjusting my coat.

Cage looked up. "So, what now?"

I smiled. "We go fishing."

For the remainder of the day, the precinct settled into its usual rhythm: ringing phones, keyboards clacking, and the low murmur of conversation—the kind of controlled chaos that made the city run, whether it liked it or not. I had just set my coffee on my desk when Hunter pulled up a chair. Not just anywhere—right next to me.

I gave her a look. "You know there's about thirty open desks over there, right?"

She shrugged, setting her own coffee down. "Yeah, but none of them are this close to the drinks station."

I leaned back, eyeing her. "So, what's on your mind?"

Hunter placed her laptop on the desk and cracked her knuckles. "Cash mentioned something about you being all worked up over Sandra again."

Damnit. "He better knock it off about my niece, or he's gonna need a dentist real soon." I met Hunter's concerned gaze and sighed. "She, uh, just graduated. They stuck her in the 27th Ward."

Hunter frowned. "That's rough."

Understatement of the year, that. The 27th Ward was a goddamn war zone. An old block. A battleground where criminals, politicians, and dirty money blurred the lines between law and lawlessness. You didn't just survive there—you chose to play the game, or you got buried by it…

I spared Hunter my internal rant and just nodded. "Yeah. And she's out there thinking she can change the damn world."

Hunter smiled. "What's wrong with that?"

I snorted. "Kid, you wanna change the world? Become a lawyer. That's how you do it."

"You saying cops don't make a difference?"

I had to laugh at that. "Do you know how many laws get passed that undo every arrest we make? How many cases get thrown out because some slick-suited jackass found a loophole?" I sighed. "Look, Sandra's smart. Hardworking. She wants to be a detective, which is already a bad enough life decision. But now she's dating some punk who's got a record. Not enough to lock him up, but enough to tell me he's got nothing to offer her."

Hunter stroked her chin. "So what's the game plan? Threaten to bury him in the woods?"

"Don't tempt me," I muttered.

She shook her head. "Maybe he's not all bad."

I shot her another look. "Well, you're welcome to him."

Hunter laughed. "I'll pass." She tapped a finger against her cup. "So, why didn't you become a lawyer then?"

"Because somebody's got to do the dirty work."

She huffed a laugh. "And you think Sandra can't handle the job?"

I shook my head. "It's not about handling it. It's about *understanding* it. The emergency system in this city is split between cops and firefighters. Between the two of us, we handle all the city's problems. Every crisis, every disaster. We are the ones who show up first. Every time."

Hunter nodded. "Two-minute response time."

I met her eyes. "Exactly. But what happens after that? What happens after we show up? We arrest, we report, and we file paperwork. And then? The system spits these assholes back out. That's why real change happens from the top down."

Hunter exhaled. "And Sandra's an idealist, it seems."

She was quiet for a beat. Then she spun her laptop toward me. "Listen, I found something on Caldwell."

I leaned in. The headline on the screen made my stomach drop: "*Grieving Military Father Refuses to Disclose Son's Burial Location.*"

I frowned. "Yeah, I've already got this."

Hunter straightened in her chair. "You do?"

I nodded, dragging a hand over my face. "You remember, I've been keeping an eye on Caldwell for years. This incident is when I started upping my surveillance. But like I said, nothing ever stuck. He's clean. Too clean."

Hunter clicked through the article. "Former Jungle Recon… Son was killed while he was deployed… No funeral, no known gravesite. No further details."

"That's what we already knew." I drummed the desk with my knuckles. "But where's the kicker?"

Hunter shook her head, then reached into the file beside her. Out came a printed photo of Lucas Bennett. Without a word, she placed it next to a picture of young Tommy Caldwell, Jr.

The resemblance hit me like a brick. Same face. Same hair. Same damn eyes.

Hunter's voice was steady. "That's not a coincidence, Dawson."

I clenched my jaw. "No. It's not."

I grabbed the file, flipping through the pages. My pulse picked up. "Alright. There's got to be something he's hiding that we can pick up. Something that went under the radar."

Hunter started running searches. "There's nothing. No traffic tickets. No property violations. Just nothing." She clicked open another screen. "All we know is he was part of Jungle Recon. We know the knife, traced it back to the platoon, but not to Tom specifically. Eleven guys in that unit could be suspects."

I nodded. "Then let's narrow it down."

She pulled up a map. "Of the eleven, only four are anywhere near the area. The others are deployed or states away. Cage is already in custody. That leaves three—Bronson, Aspen, and Caldwell."

I tapped the screen. "Commander Aspen's still active?"

"Yeah. Says he's stationed at a base a sector over. Bronson's there, too. Both are still serving."

I exhaled. "There's a few off the books."

"Print what we got," I said. "Add it to the file."

She pressed the button. The printer whirred, ejecting the image. I grabbed it, bringing it to eye level. *All these years, this guy banked on everyone thinking he was just some ex-military recluse…*

"Let's go deeper," I muttered.

Hunter started pulling military records. Commander Aspen. Bronson. Caldwell. Then—

ACCESS DENIED. A message flashed: *For further access, contact legal representative Jeffrey Weinberg.*

I scoffed. "Weinberg…"

Hunter looked up. "Who is he?"

"A lawyer. The kind of lawyer that only works for people with something to hide."

"And Caldwell hired him." She frowned. "So, what now?"

I slammed my fist on the desk so hard the monitor rattled. "What the hell kind of lawyer can block information on the internet like that?" The desperation in my voice cut through the chatter of the office. I was a damn detective, and they still found a way to cut me off at the knees. Political sabotage.

"Could be the government doing it, though." Hunter leaned back in her chair, arms crossed. "It is military information we're trying to access, after all."

"We're government, too!" I snapped. "Last I checked, the military doesn't outrank any criminal cases on Big East soil."

Hunter put her hands on her face. "Dawson, this can't just be about some street thug. This guy lawyered up. Helmsley could have his hands in it."

I shook my head. "A hurdle's only as high as you lift your damn feet."

Hunter looked at me, perplexed. "Dawson, take a breath. Let's call it a night. Think."

Think? I'd done nothing but think. And it led me nowhere.

"Where are you going?" she called as I stormed off.

I didn't answer.

CHAPTER 16

THE LUCID ENTANGLEMENT

I look at the bedside clock—1:50 AM. *What a great time, a buck and a half…*

I've had too much to drink. Don't care.I Didn't count. Just kept pouring *Villon* neat. Glass after glass, one, two, three. The walls creep in around me as my thoughts circle the same dead-end road…

My pager buzzes. Ms. Anderson. Reporters. Too many damn questions. How the hell did they get my number?

Cage's voice clawing at the back of my mind, his smug, needle-ridden smirk. *"You're old, Dawson. You don't get it anymore."* He wouldn't even look at me directly, just tossed his words like knives and laughed when they landed.

I grab my phone. The judge isn't giving me any of the warrants I requested. Good. I toss the badge onto the nightstand and grab my keys.

The engine hums low as I pull up to Tom's house. The streetlights barely reach the long driveway, shadows swallowing the place whole. My breath fogs against the windshield.

Enough is enough.

I step out, feet crunching against the gravel. No knock. No announcement. No shield of authority.

I'm not a cop anymore. Not now.

I exhale. Steady. Keep my heart rate controlled.

My fingers flex against the grip of my 357 Magnum, the metal is warm against my palm. Loaded. Chambered. Ready.

I get out of the car. The wind is almost nonexistent, the silence unsettling. *The house is watching me.*

I cross the yard, one foot in front of the other. The front door's cracked like he's been waiting. Like he wants me to walk into the trap.

But I'm not stupid.

I slide behind the stone pillar just outside the porch. Gun lowered. Eyes sharp. Listening.

Then—I breach, gun raised, screen door creaking behind me.

The game begins.

The air in the house smells like dust and gun oil. A waiting room for the dead. I cleared the left. Cleared the right. Nothing but shadows.

Then—movement. A figure on the staircase.

Tom.

I follow, straining the wooden floorboards with each step. At the top of the staircase, he is waiting.

He smirks. I spy the Jungle Recon tattoo stretched across his forearm, barely visible in the flickering light.

"Well, well," Tom drawls. "Paramilitary meets military." He spreads his arms wide. "Like what I've done with the place?"

"You know why I'm here."

Tom takes a slow step forward. "Then quit talking. Bring it."

My sunglasses—outfitted with infrared detection—pick up the Claymore tucked by the doorway. *Cute*. Not falling for that again. I step over the beam. For a second, the ground feels solid. I plant my second foot, squaring up, ready for a fight.

The smirk on Tom's face is the last thing I see before the floor gives way beneath me.

My body slips clean through the floor, my knee slamming against jagged wood. My jacket tears against the splintered edges as my arms flail, grasping for anything to grab onto…

Then—*I hit concrete.*

Pain explodes through my shoulder. The world spins, dust and dim light swirl above me.

Footsteps. Tom Caldwell.

From the edge of the hole, he looks down at me like a king admiring his kingdom. Laughing.

"You think I'd blow up my own house just for you?"

I sit up, groaning. Dazed. Confused. Pissed.

Tom's voice echoes from above. "Hey, Charlie… what takes longer—becoming a hair stylist or becoming a cop?"

My vision swims. *To hell with this guy.*

"No?" Tom cackles. "Let me help you out. Hair stylist? Two years. A cop? Nine months. And judging by how you just fell through that floor like a damn cartoon, I'd say they should've given you an extra semester…"

He spits into the hole. "*I told you not to fuck with my family.*"

I taste blood. I taste fear. Outside, someone pounds on the door. *Lucas? Jake?*

I can feel myself blacking out—my mind shutting down, slipping away…

Somewhere in the distance, I hear her voice.

"Freeze!"

Hunter. She's here.

"Keep your hands where I can see them!"

Tom sighs. With one fluid motion, he spins and disarms her. The Glock snaps in half like it's made of plastic.

I lay lifeless, helpless.

The defibrillator flashes red.

No charge. No way back.

Tom grabbed Hunter by the ankle. *Drags* her.

She reaches out—grasping for me.

"Dawson!"Blood pools beneath my head. I try to move. Nothing. I try to breathe. Nothing.

Then—

A shock. Raw. Violent. Like somebody just dropped a toaster in the bathtub.

I'd curse out Paxton if I wasn't busy convulsing.

The electricity slams through my body, snapping me back to life.

My blood rages. My veins pump. Heat coils in my chest, rolling through my limbs like I've been dunked into a vat of liquid fire.

I ripped the defibrillator's probes off, and—

—I jolted awake, seeing red. The dim glow of the digital clock burned against the darkness.

3:47 AM.

I lay in bed, gun in hand, barrel raised. The comforter hung halfway off my body, twisted like I had been fighting in my sleep. I scanned the room, every muscle coiled, ready to strike.

Clear.

My pulse pounded against my ribs as I turned toward the window. The half-empty bottle of Villon Cognac sat on the dresser, amber liquid catching the light. Sweat slicked my chest and the shiny plate of the defibrillator.

My hands were shaking. Slowly, I used the muzzle of the .357 Magnum to pull back the window shade. Thunder cracked.

Nothing. Just the city, the hum of the streets below, the distant wail of a siren.

I exhaled.

It was all a dream.

Even in my nightmares, Tom still had the upper hand.

The remnants of the dream clung to me like a second skin. Sleep wasn't coming back tonight. I reached for my phone, fingers moving on instinct, pulling up the team's group chat. For a moment, my thumbs hovered over the screen. Then, I typed:

Surveillance is still on for tomorrow morning. 0600 hours. Parking lot up the street from Elm Diner. Be ready.

I hit send.

No one would respond at this hour. Didn't matter. I closed my eyes, willed the beating of my heart to slow. To not launch me back into a mad firefight the moment I drifted off again.

Tomorrow, I told myself. Tomorrow, we'll be watching. Waiting.

And I'd be ready for it.

CHAPTER 17

THE WATCHFUL HUNT

NOVEMBER 12TH – 7:58 AM

The early morning air was crisp beneath a cold blue sky. I pulled into the lot up the street from Elm Diner, my Porsche purring low as it rolled to a stop. A moment later, a white surveillance van eased into position in the adjacent lot, Hunter behind the wheel. I climbed inside.

Before she even killed the engine, I could hear Cash inside in the back, adjusting the live surveillance feeds, his headset resting over one ear. He was good—damn good—but I needed him at his best today.

The Reconnaissance and Surveillance Tracker was running—James' brainchild, our department's top tech. This thing didn't just track real-time movement. It mapped patterns, habits, and potential next moves. It was what separated us from every other squad in the city.

Cash tapped the screen, zooming in on a black pickup truck parked near the diner. It had military decals on its rear window and a sticker.

I checked my watch. "He hits this diner three times a week," I muttered. "Hopefully, today's our lucky day."

No one spoke. I scanned the faces—Hunter, Johnston, Cash.

"You know your objectives. No interference. Earpieces in, surveillance tight." I let my gaze linger on Johnston a second longer. "No one makes a move unless I say. We're here to talk, not to start something. No scenes, no heat, no unnecessary risks."

I paused. "Stay in position. Keep your eyes open."

Cash muttered something under his breath, but I ignored it. I stepped out of the van, rolling my shoulders once to loosen the tension in my frame. A deep breath. Then, after measured steps across the parking lot, I pushed open the diner door.

Showtime.

The Big East Elm Diner smelled like coffee, bacon grease, and burnt toast—the kind of place where time never moved too fast, but the coffee always poured hot. I slid into a booth near the back, trench coat draping over the seat beside me. Sunglasses off.

The waitress poured me a mug of joe. "Gimme two of those," I told her. I stirred in sugar, speaking through the earpiece like I was teaching a class.

"Alright, team. Let me show you how to pick apart a man."

Outside, Cash stayed in the van, fingers tapping away at his laptop. Johnston would sit in the Porsche across the street, line of sight clear. Hunter headed off to park near Caldwell's house, ready to tail him the second he so much as adjusted his rearview mirror.

Surveillance 101.

"First lesson: Everybody has habits. Nobody is unpredictable. They just think they are." I sipped my coffee. "Second lesson—you let them walk into the net on their own."

Cash's voice crackled through the comms. "*Got a match on his truck. No paper trail on his credit card history. Pays in cash every time.*"

I smirked. Of course he does. "What else?"

Cash cleared his throat. "*Went in yesterday, asked around. He usually orders light. Egg white omelet, maybe a Big East sandwich. But lately? He's been doubling up. Waffles, pancakes, two full platters—the Big M's Breakfast and the Big E's Breakfast.*"

I leaned back, fingers tapping against my cup. "So, either he's feeding more people… or he's planning for something."

Outside, the diner door jingled. Tom Caldwell stepped inside. I set my coffee down, tilting my sunglasses back onto my face.

Caldwell moved like a man with purpose—back straight, steps controlled. He removed his cap as soon as he stepped in. An old military habit. Respect for the room.

"Hey, Amy. The usual, if you please."

Amy, the waitress, hesitated. Her eyes flicked toward me, occupying his usual table. "Uh… looks like someone already ordered it for you."

Caldwell's facial muscles locked in place. Without looking, I could tell he knew. A few diner patrons' heads turned, perhaps sensing the static in the air.

Through the earpiece, Cash muttered, *"Boss, I don't like this. The guy looks too comfortable…"*

"Keep the radio traffic clear," I murmured back.

Caldwell turned, his sharp eyes cutting through the diner like a scope. I tilted my chin toward the booth seat across from me. "Take a seat, Tommy. Been a long time."

He exhaled, barely a smirk on his lips, then slid into the booth. Probably the same posture he used in every interrogation room—relaxed, but ready.

"What is this, Charlie? My hero's welcome?"

I didn't even look up. Kept drinking my coffee.

He went on. "You got a parade waiting out back? Some balloons on standby?"

I finally looked up—slow, calm. "Hero?" I said. "You're no hero."

His smile twitched. "Don't come in here acting like you're clean."

I looked down at my leather jacket. Brushed a bit of lint off the sleeve. "Looks pretty clean to me, Tom."

He leaned forward, voice low. "You know what? I've been feeling challenged lately."

That was the first time I saw him grin. Not a smirk. Not a bluff. A real grin—like the devil had finally found a dance partner.

It wasn't confidence. It was bait. He wanted me to play into it. Wanted me to step off balance—just once.

But I'd already had enough of his games.

I stirred my coffee again, the spoon clinking noisily against the ceramic. "Blink once if you did it. Blink twice if you did it."

———

Caldwell chuckled. "Were you always this clever, or have you been taking lessons?"

I took another slow sip and tried not to flinch.

He smirked widely. "A miracle you have the time to come after me, hopping in and out of beds all over the city like you do."

I swallowed. Set the cup down. *So, he's been keeping tabs on me, too, huh?* "So, what? I lose my pension. No crime in that," I said. Then, I leaned forward, and—

BANG. My fist slammed onto the table, rattling the coffee saucers. "But snatching kids out of theirs? That's another thing entirely."

The diner was dead silent, the murmurs dispensed. Every ear in the room was tuned in to our exchange.

Then, a new voice cut through the moment.

"Excuse me, sir."

I turned. An old vet with a military pin on his lapel stepped forward. Navy shirt. Eyes sharp. His voice was firm. "I don't know what's going on, but you show this man some respect. He served his country."

My jaw clenched. *De-escalate.* Through gritted teeth, I said, "Yes, sir."

Caldwell barely looked at the vet. "Do I look like I need defending?"

Hunter's voice buzzed in my ear. *"Boss, Johnston's moving."*

Just caught it out of the corner of my eye—he was strafing between cars, slow, steady, like a man rehearsing something.

His hand resting on top of his service pistol.

I threw up my fist—a silent command out the diner window: *Stop. Hold the line.*

Johnston froze like a rookie who'd just seen his career flash before his eyes. *Thank God his instincts finally caught up.* He backed away.

But Caldwell saw him. He smirked, rolling his sleeves up like he was settling in for dinner and a show.

I shrugged. "Rookie nerves."

His gaze drifted outside past Johnston, toward the van. "And that must be Mr. Cash, probably still deciding between waffles and pancakes." Then he rounded on me again. "Your platoon is a joke."

That did it, I reached into my pocket and placed my vintage pocket watch on the table, and clenched my jaw. "This time next week, Tommy… You'll be in a four-by-four. Hots and a cot."

Tom barked, "Oh yeah? This time next week, huh?" He reached into his pocket. I saw a glimmer of something small, metallic.

Then—*WHACK*. He slammed a speaker magnet onto the topside of the table. The salt and pepper shakers rattled, then clattered to the floor. One cracked open, dark granules spilling across the floor like ashes.

Huh. I'd pegged this place for plastic lids. I looked down at my wrist; my pocketwatch had started spinning erratically—the hands whipping so fast my eyes couldn't follow. The speaker in my ear crackled with static. I could hear Cash's voice coming in and out indistinctly.

I grimaced and stared up at Caldwell, his face unreadable. But behind the mask?

You could see it flash across his eyes—for just a beat. He was too tactical.

I made a mental note to do some more digging on his father, once this shitshow wrapped up. Bet his mother hated them both.

Caldwell flicked the magnet onto the table with a grin. A casual toss, like it was nothing more than a toy to him. Then, he stood. Fatigues crisp. Boots military tight. Like he never left the war. He didn't rush, just turned to Amy and said, "He's paying for my coffee too, sweetheart."

Then he grabbed both bags of food and walked out of the diner.

I sat there, turning over my broken watch in my hand. Stuck on 1:08 now. I slid my sunglasses back on.

The worst ones don't foam at the mouth or rant in code. They're all logic. No emotion.

Men like Tom don't throw punches. They engineer outcomes.

Luckily, I pay attention.

NOVEMBER 13TH – 9:14 AM

The next morning, everything happened right on schedule. I was sitting at my desk, waiting for my watch to finish its repair ticket—earbuds in, sipping my burnt precinct coffee in time with some zen music—when the door of the precinct slammed open. In walked Attorney Jeffrey Weinberg. His suit was sharp, but his movements were erratic—shoulders tense, jaw clenched, sweat beading at his temple. He ignored Barbara's protests as he stormed past the front desk.

"Excuse me, sir! You can't just barge in here!"

I didn't move, just slid my coffee aside and watched Weinberg from afar as he moved deeper into the cubicle maze. Oh, Weinberg: too much mouth and not enough sense. I caught Hunter's eye. *Trespassing.*

His head snapped left, then right, one eye twitching like he hadn't slept in days. "Where the hell is Dawson?"

I stepped forward into his blustering path. He turned and smacked right into my chest, stumbling backward. Before he could recover, I shoved him down into a rolling chair. His breath hitched as the wheels screeched against the linoleum.

I loomed over him. "You lost, counselor?"

Weinberg rounded on me, red-faced as a potbelly pig. "You need to stop harassing my client, Dawson."

I looked up slowly. "The client walked into a public diner, Jeff. Sat down across from me. It's not like I chased him down."

"Don't play smart with me!" he snapped. "You think that badge makes you untouchable?"

"Not untouchable," I said. "Just correct."

Hunter appeared beside me, arms crossed. "He's not wrong. Your guy walked into the diner of his own accord. Our team just happened to be posted there. Coincidence or confession—you pick."

Weinberg's beady eyes narrowed. "I wonder what your Chief would think about you skirting the law like this."

"Don't test me, Weinberg. I'd be shaking hands with Internal Affairs and still make it home in time for dinner, and you know it."

Weinberg looked like he was about to burst. "You've got to cease this nonsense!" he snapped, pointing a shaky finger in my face. "You're crossing lines—legal ones!"

I didn't flinch. "You're already back here without clearance, Jeff. That's trespassing. I could've had you cuffed ten minutes ago."

He scoffed. "Oh, come on. You've got no right."

"*Maybe.*" I stepped closer. "But then again, maybe I'm letting you talk… seeing what you'll let slip."

His face twisted. "You don't scare me."

"That's too bad," I said. "Because you should be scared. You're one outburst away from getting locked up."

"Is that a threat?"

"No," I said, lowering my voice. "But if it was… it'd already be done."

———

He opened his mouth—then said something he realized too late he shouldn't have.

"You're all part of it… You'll see. You think this ends with me?"

And there it was. He sunk his own ship.

I turned to Hunter. "Was that a threat to hurt himself or others?"

Weinberg adjusted his tie, trying to regain some composure. "You're twisting my words."

I tilted my head. "Twisting?" I let the word hang for a moment, then narrowed my eyes. "For a second there, it almost sounded like you're having suicidal ideations."

His face drained of color. "No—what? Of course I didn't mean—"

Hunter stepped up beside me, shaking her head. "Damn, Jeff. That's a serious concern. Maybe you should be evaluated."

"No, no, no," he snapped, shaking his head, panic creeping into his voice. "That's not what I meant."

I crouched down, leveling my gaze with his. "It doesn't matter what you meant. What matters is what we heard. And lucky for you… we take mental health and safety seriously."

Weinberg's breath quickened. I tapped my radio. "Hunter, what's the call for an involuntary psych evaluation?"

She smirked. "That'd be a 36, boss."

I clicked my radio. "Dispatch, I got a 36 at the precinct. Send the 29s. I need him on watch."

The radio crackled. "*Copy that. Uniformed officers en route.*"

Weinberg's head snapped up. "What the hell are you talking about?"

Within moments, footsteps echoed down the hall. Two uniformed patrol officers entered, their expressions blank, professional.

"Attorney Weinberg," I said, stepping back. "You're not well. We want to preserve your public image. So, we're going to take you in through the back. No media, no unnecessary attention."

The officers moved in, securing cuffs to his wrists.

"No, no, wait a damn minute—"

"Relax, counselor." Hunter patted his shoulder mockingly. "This is for your protection."

The officers hoisted him up, leading him toward the back exit.

Weinberg struggled. "You can't do this! I'll have your badges for this!"

I shrugged, sliding my hands into my pockets. "Sure you will."

As the doors closed behind him, I turned to Hunter.

She raised an eyebrow. "Three days sedated. Locked up. You really think he's going to talk after that?"

"I don't need him to talk. I just need him to suffer."

CHAPTER 18

ALONE IN THE DARK

Oliver came to in fragments.

The air hit him first—thick, wet, foul. There was mildew soaked into the walls, rust in the pipes, and the unmistakable scent of dried blood emanating from the floor, like an invisible stain no mop could lift. His head pounded, and his stomach rolled.

From above—heavy footsteps. Voices. Something scraping. I'm in a basement, he realized. Then came the creak.

The door opened.

Light bled in from a stairway—and a man filled the frame. Big. Solid. Like he was carved out of cinderblocks. He moved toward Oliver with quiet purpose.

Oliver blinked. Tried to rise. The man walked in and crouched beside him.

"You had a mild concussion," said Tom Caldwell. "I stitched you up—yeah, they're a little crooked. But I learned to sew flesh in a combat zone, and in places like that, straight lines stop mattering."

Oliver jerked back, panic tightening in his chest. "Don't touch me."

"Let me check that bruise—"

"You better back up off me!"

Tom's eyes narrowed, voice dropping an octave. "Fine then. Bleed to death." He stood up , towering over Oliver. Then, a crazed gleam flashed across his eyes. "You kids think this is a game? Spreading havoc all over the damn town? You know what I was doing while you were out cold?"

He stepped forward, jabbing a finger toward Oliver. "I was cleaning dog shit off my porch. That's your idea of fun?"

Oliver didn't answer. Tom kept going, voice rising to a slow boil.

"You skipped every house on the block—every damn driveway. You just had to climb the hill, all the way up to my house. Just to smear crap on my doorstep and throw toilet paper in my trees?"

He let that hang in the air. "You got some nerve." Tom leaned in again, his voice now like cold steel. "And now I'm down here… trying to help you."

Oliver's jaw clenched. "W-where's Lucas?"

Tom's eyes locked on his. "You'll see him soon."

"Is he okay?"

"You're safe," Tom said. "*He's* not."

That landed like a punch to the chest.

Tom stepped back, arms crossed. "You think ringing my bell was some harmless dare? You kicked down a door you can't close."

Oliver swallowed. "What do you want?"

Tom didn't answer. Not right away. He paced once around the basement—slowly, deliberately—then stopped.

"Whose idea was it?"

Oliver's mouth twitched. "It-it was mine."

Tom gave a small, cruel smile. "Well… lucky for Lucas, you brought him to the right place." Tom started up the stairs.

At the bottom step, he turned back. "You've got one job, boy: Sit still. Heal up. Don't make me regret not leaving you out cold on the sidewalk." He twitched, muttering as he climbed the steps,

Then he was gone. The door slammed. Locks turned.

Darkness swallowed the room again.

CHAPTER 19

THE ARCHITECTS OF CONTROL

NOVEMBER 13TH – 3:55 PM

The Alderman's Chambers existed on the border between two worlds. Inside, on the first floor, the staff moved in and out like busy bees, efficient, orderly. Outside, however, the clatter of camera equipment was the soundtrack of mayhem. Flashbulbs popped as the Mayor made his way toward the entrance through the sea of reporters, flanked by security.

"Mayor Dickerson, any comments on the recent kidnappings?"

"Mr. Mayor, crime is skyrocketing—"

A microphone was practically shoved in John Dickerson's face. He adjusted his tie and sighed, his irritation barely masked by rehearsed calm. "The city is overblown right now, yes, but don't worry. We'll meet today so we can handle it tomorrow."

"Mayor! Protesters are camping outside the courthouse…"

———

He barely glanced backward. "We'll handle that too, six a.m. sharp. Ms. Rose, you and your crew will be there, right?"

Kelsey gave a curt nod, already calling off her dogs.

The Mayor didn't wait for another question. He moved into the building, and by the time he and his entourage reached the second floor, he found his mood had improved.

The Alderman's Chambers were dimly lit, lined with portraits of those who had come before, men who once held the city in their grip. Lingering on the shelves was the smell of old books, polished wood, and faint cigar smoke, relics of deals made behind these very doors.

At the top of the stairs, Judge Alex Helmsley stood waiting, his robe slung over his arm. His usual courtroom authority seemed stripped down to something weaker, more personal.

The Alderman—Robert Capello, the smooth-talking politician—coughed. "Gentlemen. In my office. Now."

Inside, the microphones were pushed aside. The public didn't get to hear this part. This was where the city was run. They each took their seats, the unspoken power structure forming automatically.

A few minutes later, in staggered Jeffrey Weinberg, the most influential lawyer in the city, the one who could make sure certain people stayed out of prison.

"God *damn* that Dawson…" Weinberg sputtered, smoothing down his wrinkled tie and combing over his tousled crop of hair. "…Tries to have me committed… better watch his back…"

At last, he took his seat at the mahogany table. Together, these five—mayor, judge, alderman, preacher, and lawyer—were the ones who decided how things worked in The Big East.

And tonight, things weren't working.

The Mayor leaned back, his fingers steepled in front of him. "Gentlemen, gentlemen, gentlemen…" He let the words fall like the first drops before a storm. "We need to get this situation under control. Fast."

Capello wasn't having it. "Hey, hey, you're not a lame duck, Dick," he shot back, his voice edged with mockery and frustration.

The Mayor's eyes narrowed. "Someone's setting this city on fire, and you didn't even try to put it out."

The Judge gave a slow, deliberate nod, tapping the briefcase at his side. "Gentlemen," he said, his voice smooth, almost bored, "let's get down to business."

But the Mayor wasn't done. His hand came down hard on a stack of crime reports, sending papers flying. "Your backdoor policies and decisions have finally come to a head. And now—now we're facing the consequences." His eyes locked on Capello, whose jaw clenched in return.

Capello leaned in. Unshaken. "The bill was about compassion. Addressing the root causes of crime. You think locking people up is the answer?"

The Judge's laugh was sharp, almost cruel. "In that case, we may as well lock up the whole damn building, Capello."

The Mayor didn't flinch. "Compassion doesn't excuse chaos. You tied the hands of the police, crime is up, people are scared, and now the streets are running with blood. And I don't mean metaphorically. You gave criminals an inch, and they're taking *miles*."

Weinberg spoke, his voice laced with contempt. "We got cops like Dawson thinking they run this city, and they don't." He scoffed, shaking his head. "That bastard and his crew tried to lock me up in a psych ward for thirty-six hours." His face dropped into a bitter sneer. "*Fuck* Dawson. Fuck his whole crew."

The Preacher finally spoke up, his voice like silk. "Let's talk about overcrowding," he murmured. "We don't solve this by stuffing more men into cages. We need programs, education, guidance."

The Judge's face hardened. "And what do you propose, Preacher?" he challenged. "Tell me, do you believe that good people commit crimes? Do you think soft laws will fix a broken city? What is this, 'Defund the Police'? *Please.*"

The Preacher smiled, slow and knowing. "Those who defend evil shall perish." His voice had weight, sinking into the walls like scripture written in blood. He stood, raising his hands like he was giving a sermon.

"Brethren, we stand at the crossroads. Our city bleeds, pleading for salvation—not further damnation."

Capello shifted in his seat. Weinberg's gaze darkened. The men sat in this room, full of doubts, while silence settled around them, thick as cigar smoke.

The Mayor adjusted his tie, his fingers smoothing over the silk as he leaned forward. He was the last word in this room, always had been.

"We will not demonize our first responders," he said, his voice steady, assured. "We can't sit back and let them be blamed for the pressures that we neglected." His eyes flicked to the Judge, Capello, the Preacher, and Weinberg, daring them to challenge him. "Bring calm, fellas. If we play our cards right, everything's going to blow over."

NOVEMBER 16TH – 11:20 AM

It always starts the same way.

People get angry. They gather, they chant, they press against the barricades. Then something breaks.

And once it breaks, it never goes back.

The sun had barely hit the skyline, but the city was already teeming with life—and fury. The streets swelled with bodies, packed shoulder to shoulder. Their voices weren't just noise—they were a force, pressing hard against the walls of City Hall.

Handmade signs stabbed the air over the throng: *BRING OUR KIDS HOME!*

NO JUSTICE, NO PEACE!

MAYOR DICK IS A DICK!

The riot cops held the line, but just barely, as the ambulances, fire trucks, and first responders moved into position—ready to deal with the aftermath.

I weaved forward through the shifting crowd, Hunter beside me. I could feel the energy crackling in the air, wild and unsteady. Somewhere ahead, a protester locked eyes with me.

He stepped forward. "Every forty seconds, a child disappears in this country. That figure goes up thirty-five percent around Halloween. How many more, Detective?"

I didn't blink. Hunter stepped in, her voice steady. "We've been working day and night to ensure these streets are safe."

The protester shook his head, hands clenched into fists. "It's been too many nights."

Behind us, the barricades trembled. The riot cops shifted, bracing to be overrun.

Hunter elbowed me. "This is bad."

I scanned the crowd. "This is a damn war zone." And just as the words left my mouth—

Boom. A trash can exploded.

Flames punched into the air. Metal and debris scattered across the pavement. Smoke billowed upward, twisting in the wind, and was carried straight toward City Hall.

The barricades continued to shake. Someone shoved. Someone pushed back. A bottle flew overhead, shattering green glass against the courthouse steps.

And then the line broke.

The crowd surged. Riot shields slammed backward. A cop went down, her baton skidding across the pavement. Tear gas erupted, so that noxious white clouds curled through the street, swallowing everything whole.

I yanked my collar up over my mouth, throat burning. Hunter sputtered beside me, eyes red. Through the thick haze, though, I managed to spot it: a black SUV pulling up fast.

Dickerson.

The moment his car door opened, dozens of necks craned to get a glimpse of the Mayor. The crowd shifted to start hurling their pleas at him.

Mayor Dickerson stepped out, slick as ever, adjusting his tie like he was stepping into a press conference instead of a battlefield.

He didn't hurry. Didn't flinch. Didn't acknowledge the rage swallowing the street. His security detail closed in tight, ready to haul him back inside if things went sideways.

If you asked me, he enjoyed hearing the people scream his name. Letting them feel like they had power. That's what made him dangerous.

Then, *CRACK*. A brick sailed through the air. The windshield of his SUV crunched into a spiderweb of glass. The crowd roared.

The Mayor's security detail swarmed him, but he still didn't move very quickly, considering. He just turned his head, as if assessing the damage to his vehicle for the insurance claim.

At last, calm as a cucumber, he made his way into the building.

12:31 PM

Though the streets burned, City Hall stayed frosty cold. The lobby was packed with protesters and reporters alike, all waiting on the press conference to begin, yet silence prevailed. The flashing cameras cast long shadows against the polished granite floors.

Mayor Dickerson stood at the podium, composed. His hands rested on the edges, fingers barely curling like he was in complete control.

Abruptly, one reporter's voice sliced through the quiet. "Dan Thompson, On Scene News. Mayor Dickerson, what measures are being taken to address the spike in child kidnappings?"

Dickerson's fingers drifted across the Bible in front of him. He let the silence sit. Then, smooth as glass—

"Let us begin with a moment of reflection."

His gaze swept the room as he began to recite. "Let the little children come to me, and do not hinder them, for the kingdom of God belongs to such as these."

A murmur of tepid approval passed through the crowd. Dickerson almost smiled.

Dan Thompson, however, leaned forward. "Faith doesn't find the missing, Mayor. People want action, not platitudes."

A second journalist jumped in. "Edie Pilot, Channel 7. Mayor, our police force is stretched thin. There's no end in sight."

Dickerson exhaled, tilting his head like he was carrying the weight of the world. "Our actions will reflect our commitment to justice."

Dan didn't let up. "Four of the eight kidnapped children who were found were missing organs. One was missing a hand."

At that, the room snapped. Gasoline meets fire. A voice from the back, raw with grief.

"Man, fuck this!"

Something flew. A water bottle.

It slammed into the Mayor's shoulder. He staggered, catching himself against the podium. For the first time in his public life, his face twisted—not in sorrow, not in concern, but in anger. "*You mother—!*"

But his voice vanished under the roar of the crowd. Protesters rushed forward, past the velvet ropes. Security lunged, dragging the Mayor away just in time.

Two detectives fought their way to the stage through the crush of bodies. "CLEAR A PATH!"

Dan Thompson's voice cut in through the madness, mic in hand, facing his station's cameras: "Another day in paradise."

CHAPTER 20

A CELEBRATION OF VALOR

NOVEMBER 16TH – 7:30 PM

The precinct was buzzing louder than usual. Laughter mixed with the scent of burnt coffee, printer paper, and sweat, the kind of camaraderie you only get after making it through hell together. Usually, it was us-versus-them, but right now, it was just us, cracking jokes and trading stories—fatal crashes, freak accidents, loved ones lost to the job—because the alternative was drowning in the truth.

In this world, some drank, some isolated, some handed in the badge before it even got scuffed. But my team? They were going to make it.

Don't get me wrong, I still didn't want a partner. But these ones, I hated to admit, were growing on me. And they'd earned a breather.

Now, the rookies were in rare form—riding the high of a job well done. Johnston weaved through the bullpen like a kid on Christmas morning, cradling a big box wrapped in shiny paper.

I didn't bother looking up from my desk, as I had a long-standing policy against surprises.

But the rookies didn't know that.

"Easy, kid," I muttered as Johnston plopped the giant box on my desk. "Tell me that wasn't ticking when you picked it up."

Johnston smirked. "That might be the least of your worries today."

Barbara, on the phone at the front desk, rolled her eyes, then put her hand over the receiver. "Whatever you're up to, I'm not involved," she shouted.

Before I could protest any further, a voice startled me.

"*Uncle Charlie.*" A voice I'd know anywhere.

My head snapped up, and there she was—Sandra. In uniform. *Police* uniform.

For a second, everything around me disappeared—the precinct, the rookies, the case files spread across my desk like a smorgasbord. All I saw was the kid I helped raise, standing there looking like she belonged here. Like she'd been born for this.

"Sweetheart," I exhaled, standing up. "What the hell are you doing here?"

"Thought you'd be proud." She flashed a grin. "First week on the job."

I pulled her into a hug, tighter than I intended. "Was hoping you'd be a ballerina," I mumbled, patting her back. "Now you want to chase perps and Zoom-heads through O Block?"

She smirked. "Learned from the best."

Hunter, ever the intruder, sauntered over and leaned against my desk. "Let's just hope she doesn't inherit your driving skills."

That got the whole room laughing. Even eavesdropping, Barbara cracked a smile.

Then Cash clapped his hands together. "Alright, alright, let's move this along."

Johnston cleared his throat, puffing out his chest like he was about to deliver a presidential address. "Not just any occasion, people. Let's talk about Charles Dawson: legendary detective, cracked more cold cases than anyone in department history, bodyguard to the stars—"

I shot him a look. "Bodyguard to the stars? Kid, you make it sound like I was rolling with Hollywood's finest."

Johnston grinned. "You're kind of a legend, boss."

"Legends are for storybooks," I muttered.

Hunter's voice softened. "Charlie, you've earned this."

Sandra stepped forward, gesturing toward the table. "Time for the grand unveiling."

Johnston yanked off the lid of the cake box with a flourish. "Your most recent takedown—immortalized in sugar."

I stared at the ridiculous, over-the-top image of myself drawn in icing, standing over a perp in a textbook arrest pose. Someone had even gotten the baker to pipe a little Mayor Dickerson in pink icing, wailing fat tears in the background.

Barbara finally joined us and slapped me on the back. "Twenty-five years, Dawson. You're practically part of the furniture."

I shook my head. "Christ, Barb, if you washed your face, you might get locked out of your own cell phone."

Barbara crossed her arms. "Watch it now, old man." The bullpen was in stitches

Then, against my better judgment—moved, perhaps, by all the cheesy camaraderie, or maybe by Sandra standing there in that uniform—I clinked my fork against my coffee mug. The precinct quieted.

I rubbed an awkward hand over my stubble. "I ain't one for speeches," I began. "You all know that. But today feels different."

Some of the officers nodded, raising their own coffee cups.

"When I started this job, I thought it was simple: Catch the bad guys, lock 'em up. But you learn fast that this job ain't black and white. It *takes* from you. Beats you down. Makes you wonder if you're making a damn bit of difference…"

I looked around at all these faces. At Cash and Johnston, already with slices of cake on paper plates. At Hunter, leaning in to whisper with Sandra, the two of them smiling conspiratorially.

"I've seen good men fall. I've carried partners out of situations that should've killed them. I've watched this city eat people alive." I paused, remembering. "We had a rough start, this department. Hell, it's still rough. We fight battles on the streets, and now we're fighting battles in the system. They want to defund us. Strip us of the ability to do what we do. They say we're the problem."

My voice dropped lower. "But when shit hits the fan, who do they call?"

A few voices called out in answer. "*Us.*"

"We don't do this job for thanks. We don't do it for glory. We do it for the people who have no one else fighting for them. The ones who go missing in the cracks. The ones society forgets."

My gaze landed again on Sandra. "And we do it for the ones who come after us." I clenched my jaw, forcing my voice steady. "I look around this room, and I see the best damn officers this city has. You take the hits, you get back up, and you keep going. You protect this city even when it doesn't protect you."

I raised my cup. "So yeah, this job takes from you. But it gives something back, too. It gives you family."

A deep breath. "It gives you people who will bleed for you, fight for you, drag you out of the fire, and throw themselves into it if it means you get to see another day." I straightened up, rolling my shoulders back.

"*To the job.* To the ones who've fallen. To the ones still standing. And to the ones coming up next."

The precinct erupted in applause. I let it go on a second before waving it off. "*Alright.* Enough of this soft shit. We've got work to do."

9:16 PM

After the cake was gone, and the hoorahs had concluded, and the general churning of the precinct returned to its usual pace, I leaned back in my chair, surveying my squad. Johnston was already back to running his mouth. Hunter elbowed him, while Cash told some wild-ass story.

But me? My mind was already drifting elsewhere, to someone not present with whom I might share the day's victories. I reached for my phone.

My thumb hovered over her name. Kelsey Rose.

I hesitated, only for a second. Then, I typed: You up?

A few seconds passed before she wrote back.

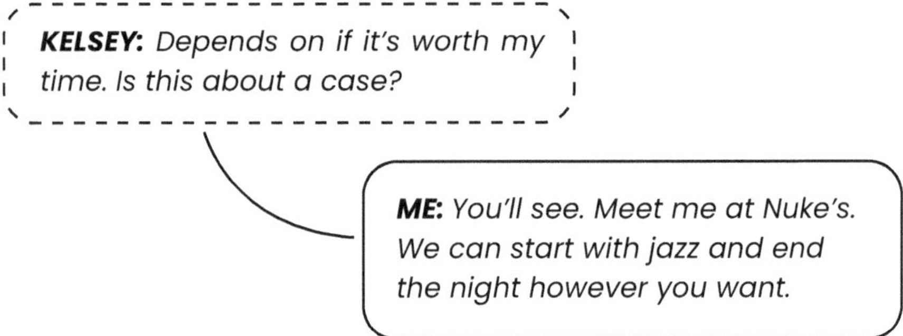

A pause. Three dots blinked while she typed her reply

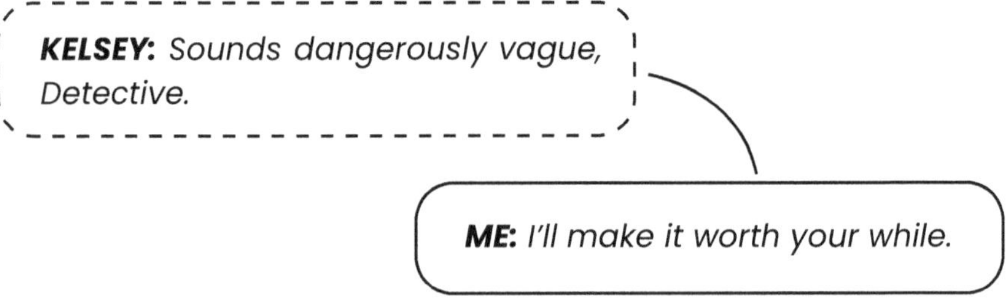

Her next reply came fast.

I locked my phone, slid it into my pocket, and rose from the table.

Hunter smirked. "Looks like someone's got plans." Cash whistled.

I shrugged into my jacket and grabbed my keys. "Try not to burn the place down."

10:05 PM

Tonight, it felt like the start of something I hadn't let myself want in a long time.

I pulled up to Nuke's, my Porsche humming low as it eased against the curb. For the first time in a while, I wasn't thinking about the city. My fingers slid over the cuffs of my sleeves, adjusting them absentmindedly.

The jazz from inside bled into the street, a smooth bass line rolling through the warm night air, laced with the scent of wine and roses. This place had a reputation. It wasn't just another lounge—it was where power huddled in the dim glow of golden sconces, where secrets were passed over glasses of Louis XIII, and where the men who ran this city knew they could disappear into something dangerous.

I stepped out of the car, rolling my shoulders as I scanned the sidewalk. Then, I saw her.

Kelsey. Leaning against the railing, bathed in soft neon, the street noise dulled in her wake. She wore a little black number, something that clung in all the right places, that made time slow down. But it wasn't just the dress that got me; it was the way she held herself in it—strong, sharp, like a blade wrapped in silk.

Her eyes found mine, the hint of a smirk playing at her lips. My phone buzzed in my pocket. I didn't need to check it.

When she stepped forward, her perfume hit me first—something warm and laced with danger. "Detective," she murmured.

"Ms. Rose." I held the door open as she stepped into the club.

Inside was all atmosphere: lights dim and golden, crystal glasses on mahogany booths, the soft hum of intimate conversation layered over the deep, rolling bass of a jazz trio.

The singer, Alana, according to a poster on the wall—slunk around the stage in an emerald dress, making her look like liquid jade. She sang: "*Under the moonlight, under the moonlight, baby, don't let go…*"

Kelsey nodded toward the stage. "You a fan?"

"Certainly sets the mood." I smirked, my hand finding the small of her back. "Let's see if it works in my favor."

Her brow lifted. "Cocky."

"Confident."

The host led us to a secluded corner booth tucked into the glow of sweet-scented candles. At the center of the table, red wine and rose petals, as requested during my hasty call on the way over from the precinct.

Kelsey slid into her seat, running a slow finger across the rim of her wine glass. "This standard at Nuke's, or is this one of your tricks?"

I leaned in to pour her merlot. "Maybe it's the first time I've done it right."

She took a sip, and the candlelight caught the gold bracelet around her wrist. "Smooth, Detective."

I tipped my own glass toward her. "You don't even know the half of it."

On stage, the violinist stole the lead from the vocalist. The melody shifted—slower, even more intimate, laced with both sorrow and anticipation.

Kelsey eyed my foot tapping and smiled. "Care for a dance, Detective?"

"You sure you can keep up?"

She stood. And I followed. She grabbed my hand and led me through the little crowd, and we found an open space near the band. The music curled around us, coaxing, teasing.

We swayed together in our game of patience.

The violin's bow arced a searing note, and the tempo jumped. The bassist grinned wide and the pianist slammed on the keys, throwing fire into the air.

Kelsey turned and shimmied, her back pressed into my chest for half a second before she spun out of reach. I caught her hand and pulled her back into my arms.

She laughed, falling into my lead. No, she didn't just follow—she met me there, matched me, challenged me.

By the time the song ended, we were breathless, for more reasons than one.

"Your car?" There was golden gravel in my voice.

Kelsey tilted her chin up. "Over there." Then smiled.

And that was all I needed.

11:48 PM

My apartment door clicked shut.

Hands found skin. Lips found breath. Clothes whispered their way off our bodies and to the floor.

I pulled Kelsey into the shower, and the heat of the cascading water banished the night's chill, steam curling around us. Water danced over her curves, down her spine, as my hands followed.

Her breath hitched as my fingers dug into her waist, her body melting against me. She caught me glancing toward the gun resting on my crumpled shirt—always within reach.

"Ever the detective," she murmured.

"Can't be too careful."

She smirked. "I could kill you right now."

I leaned in, my mouth brushing the shell of her ear. "You could try…"

She kissed me instead.

November 17th – 6:04 AM

Come morning, I jolted awake, my body tensing before my mind could catch up.

Sunlight filtered into my room through the curtains, golden streaks kissing the tangled sheets. Kelsey lay flat on her stomach, dark hair fanned across the pillow.

The nightstand was extra cluttered—bottles of Luc Belaire Luxe, one tilted on its side, the other nearly empty.

For once, everything was still. Then—

Rrrrring.

Once. Twice. Again.

On the third ring, my fingers were already reaching for my gun. I climbed carefully out of the sheets, still tangled around Kelsey, her breathing slow and peaceful. She didn't stir.

Lucky.

I crept into the bathroom and answered the phone. "Dawson."

"Charlie, we got something." It was James. *"It's bad."*

I fished my pants off the floor and started getting dressed. "Talk to me."

"A tracker. GPS. Embedded inside a stray. We ran it. It's linked to a wiped address in West Bensingworth."

My pulse picked up. "You sure?"

"Ran it through the animal database. It's a match. But here's the thing—these trackers are usually attached to a residential house. Someone scrubbed it clean and reprogrammed it."

That made me pause. A tracker like that should've led us to a home, maybe a safe house… I tightened my grip on the phone.

James hesitated. *"I expected something different when I ran it in reverse, but this… "If that's the case, it's not random. It's calculated."*

My jaw clenched. Someone was playing games. "Send me everything you've got."

7:19 AM

Hunter was already waiting outside the precinct when I pulled up, having taxied to retrieve my Porsche from outside the club. I exited and leaned against the hood, arms crossed.

I was glad when I realized I didn't need to ask if she was ready. Hunter was always ready. She slid into the passenger seat.

"Let's go, kid."

We took off, just her, me, and the hum of the engine as we carved through the city, pushing toward Bensingworth Bridge. As we got closer, the skyline shifted. The towering glass and concrete faded, replaced by older structures. Steel. Rust. Brick. The bridge loomed ahead, growing bigger, swallowing the dawn.

Train tracks cut through the underbelly of the city like an open vein, the pulse of the Bensingworth line running diagonally beneath the bridge.

And with trains came the ghosts. Homeless encampments littered the area, clusters of makeshift tents and abandoned shopping carts lining the concrete jungle. Here, the air was all stale smoke, damp earth, and cooking oil.

Then, flashing red and blue.

The crime scene unfolded like a living nightmare. The flickering yellow tape. The murmurs of forensic teams. The camera flashes—lightning in a storm of the dead.

I killed the engine. Stepped out. My boots crunched in the dirt, like old bones breaking.

Hunter whistled low under her breath. "What the hell are we walking into?" A uniformed officer lifted the tape as we ducked underneath.

Paxton, our forensics guy, was kneeling over something. A small box.

I felt my stomach tighten.

"Bomb squad cleared it," a CSI agent informed me. "It's safe."

"Go ahead," I said, my voice edged with ice. "Open our gift." Hunter shifted beside me while Paxton carefully lifted the lid.

She gagged. Her hand flew to her mouth. Too late.

Protein shake for breakfast? I almost quipped, but thought better of it. I'd seen worse.

Inside the box, neatly placed, was a severed, adult hand. In its grasp —a piece of paper that read: Luke 19:27.

I exhaled sharply, my stomach tightening into a vice. *A very familiar verse.*

"Now, as for those enemies of mine who did not want me as their king, bring them here and slay them before me…"

Hunter was still catching her breath. "Jesus *Christ*…"

I stared at the hand, then at the verse. My pulse ticked once. Twice. Then, I got it. I looked up toward the sky, puffing out a humorless laugh. "Now they want to bring God into this?"

Hunter wiped her mouth. "What does it mean?"

I didn't answer. Instead, I looked around. The area was deserted. No cameras. No street lights overhead. Only dots of neon in the distance, the dull roar of a train thundering above us.

I nodded slowly. "Whoever left this knew the area." I turned, calling out to James over the radio. "Gather everything—prints, fibers, anything that might give us a lead. This scripture isn't random. It's a challenge."

James responded: "*You think they're taunting us?*"

"They're playing chess, not checkers."

Hunter frowned. "Tell me."

I turned to her, sighing. "If you want to test a man, you test his instincts." I tapped my badge. "If you want to *break* a man, you go after his family." Then, I pointed to the hand. "But if you want to turn a man into a monster?" My jaw clenched. "You make it *personal.*"

Hunter swallowed hard. I looked at the box again, then at the crime scene. The bridge. The tracks. The emptiness.

I inhaled deeply.

"Let's see how far the ripple goes."

CHAPTER 21

FILES AND FRUSTRATIONS

NOVEMBER 19TH – 2:25 PM

My desk was a warzone—scattered folders, crime scene photos, and an empty coffee cup that had lost its fight against time. The precinct thrummed around me, static voices over dispatch, the occasional bark of a pissed-off sergeant. It was more than the usual chaos, so I found it difficult to put all my focus on the puzzle in front of me.

Across the room, Hunter leaned against a filing cabinet, arms crossed. Johnston and Cash sat nearby, whispering about the latest case—a tangled mess with no clear thread.

Then, the door creaked open. Barbara walked in with a look that told me I wouldn't like whatever she was about to say. One hand held a folder—the other, a remote control. She cleared her throat.

"Miss Dobbs just called. She's on-scene with the media."

I looked up, my chest tightening. If Natalie had headed there straight away without calling in first, that could only mean something awful had gone down. Carnage. "What are you talking about, Barbara?"

She pointed to the TV. "A man named Luther-something, they said. It's all over the news. You didn't see it?" She clicked the remote, and the screen flickered to life.

A grainy crime scene. Yellow tape whipping in the wind. Tire marks burned into the pavement. A body lying motionless on the ground—covered, but still, horrific. Death never looked surprising, just permanent.

The news anchor's voice droned over the footage.

"…a young man was found dead late last night in the industrial district. The victim, Luther Goodens, otherwise known to his associates as 'Clink', is believed to have ties to local gangs…"

My stomach hardened. *Clink.* Hadn't I heard that name before? "He's gotta be one of those punks, runs with…Kordell's crew." My eyes flicked back to Barbara. "Why the hell wasn't I informed sooner?"

She held her ground. "You were on the other case, boss. You'd just finished tracking down the kid's missing hand under the bridge."

I closed my eyes and sighed. "We didn't track down a goddamn thing."

Hunter pushed off the cabinet, stepping closer. "The timing can't be a coincidence, can it? What if, somehow, there's a connection? Between all of it…"

Johnston leaned forward, eyes sharp. "Kordell, that's who you said? We should talk to this gang, then." Cash nodded.

I flipped open the folder Barbara had handed me, rifling through the pages until I landed on the crime scene photo. Clink's lifeless body. The fresh tire tracks next to him.

Execution.

This wasn't just a body drop. This was a statement.

I tapped the edge of the folder against my desk. "We're chasing ghosts here. First, a microchipped dog that's registered to nowhere. A knife, a bloody dog tag. Then, a hand under the bridge."

Hunter leaned in. "Don't forget the note."

I nodded. "Luke 19:27. Bring my enemies here and slay them before me…"

The room went silent. As I thought, trying to pierce this mystery lurking just beneath the surface, my mind became a chessboard, every case a move, every lead a calculated step. Something was off.

Someone *else* was making moves.

I leaned back in my chair. Not convinced. "Listen," I said, rubbing my forehead, "I'm handing you over to Johnston. He's following up on the Miss Anderson file. Coordinate with him."

I gestured to Johnston, who got up and grabbed the phone. "Aye, aye, sir."

As he walked off, I stood and moved toward the weapons rack. Grabbed my revolver from the shelf. My bomber jacket hung nearby, patches of pride stitched into the fabric. I slipped it on, feeling the weight of what would come next. "Cash."

He looked up. "Boss?"

"Keep tabs on Samantha—Caldwell's ex-wife. A long-shot, but she might be key to this mess."

Cash nodded. "Got it."

Then, Hunter smirked before I could even say it. "Yeah, I know. I'm coming with you."

I stopped her with a look. "No, you're not."

She blinked. "Excuse me?"

I unholstered my gun. "Listen. I need to make some connections. Keep certain doors open."

She folded her arms. "What the hell does that mean?"

I exhaled. "It means going alone." I knew this was going to piss her off. "I'm heading into FNO territory."

Her eyes sharpened. "The hell you are."

"I have to." I grabbed my keys. "Someone's pulling the strings, and someone else is throwing rocket fuel on the fire."

Hunter stepped in front of me. "And you don't think I can handle it?"

I smirked. "Not like this."

Her jaw clenched, becoming more like me every day. Less academy, more do-or-die.

"Hunter." My voice dropped. "These thugs, they just lost one of their soldiers. This isn't a game—it's a ripple effect. The streets are about to blow, and we gotta stop it before it gets worse."

She held my gaze for a long moment. Then, finally, she let out a frustrated breath. She didn't like it, but she understood. She returned to her desk.

———

I pulled off my sports jacket, tossing it onto the chair behind me. The badge around my neck? Unclipped, hooked to my belt like an afterthought. I wouldn't need it where I was going.

Instead, I reached for the coat that spoke to who I was before the badge. Buttery-soft leather, varsity-style sleeves. A statement. A reminder. It fit like a second skin, molding to me like it had been waiting for this moment. I slid my revolver into a reverse cowboy holster, adjusting the weight until it felt right. My sunglasses followed, a slight tilt, not for style but for purpose.

I stepped out into the night, the cold air biting my face. A gang member gets dropped, and now the whole neighborhood's on edge… Kordell and his boys—they're not waiting for justice. That's not how it works in their world. Somebody's already picking targets, lining up bodies, and if I didn't get in front of it, the streets will handle this the way they always do—fast, messy, and with no regard for who pulled the trigger.

Everybody's looking for blood.

CHAPTER 22

A LINE ONCE CROSSED

NOVEMBER 19TH – 7:53 PM

The alley was shrouded in darkness, with only the streetlights shining through at a distance. The night air was cool, and Kordell's breath came out in mist as his eyes became used to the diminished light. Smothered with shadows, while graffiti-stained walls loomed like silent spectators. Dumpsters stood at fixed intervals, permeating an almost palpable stench.

Beside him, J-Rock clenched his jaw, the muscle twitching with barely contained fury. Taurese's fingers drummed against his thigh, betraying the tension coursing through him.

"Look who it is." Volume masked the caution in Kordell's voice.

A jeering snarl came out of the dark, and before them appeared a delegation from a rival gang, its members' scowls their suits of armor, their collective bravado a refusal to bend to the coming darkness.

"This ain't your turf, is it?" the gang leader sneered, cutting like a knife through the chill of the night. "Didn't think you had the guts."

J-Rock's response came fast- a warning shot flung from the stew of his rage. "Watch it," he growled, the words thick with threat.

The rival spat. "Man, respect? Clink spent his last days snatching purses from people who couldn't even chase him."

"Keep his name out yo mouth," Kordell said .

But the opposing gang laughed, their mockery echoing through the silence like cruel bells.

"Are you part of what happened to Clink?" Kordell asked .

The laughter faltered and fell, replaced by heavy silence. J-Rock's eyes never once strayed from the rival gang, eyes emanating a barely contained madness. "He was somebody to us," he spat. "And if I find out you had anything to do with it, you're gonna wish you hadn't."

Suddenly, a flash of metal gleamed in the dim light. It was a gun thrusted forward by one of the rival gang members, pointed at Jay Rock's head. It glinted ominously in the cold air.

"Scared yet?" the rival leader mocked, his words dripping with malice.

But J-Rock didn't flinch, his hand shaking only a little—a challenge to the rival gang to make their move.

"Pops gone, moms on drugs!" he yelled out in a shrill voice that echoed through the alleyways. "Please, do it! Do it! You got balls?"

Kordell's voice cut through the mayhem with desperation, pleading, "J-Rock!"

But J-Rock stood firm, his body resolute in his disagreement. "I got this!" he yelled into the night, challenging the universe to break him.

The rival gang didn't know what to make of this display of raw emotion. Their weapons fell , smugness blinking out of their eyes.

Time seemed to stand still. A car engine backfired way off in the distance. The men listened to the heavy breathing of Kordell and Taurese, whose bodies went rigid, their eyes fixed on J-Rock's defiant stance.

Then, one of the opposing members muttered, "Enough." With a soft click of his weapon, the leader stepped backward, followed by the others.***

Later that night, Kordell and his crew walked for miles, out of enemy territory and back into their turf. Back to the memorial again, because Clink had been one of them. He deserved their reverence, their sorrow.

But what they found wasn't closure—it was devastation. His memorial, once a sacred ground, was destroyed.

J-Rock's breath hitched, his throat tightening as his eyes locked onto the wreckage. His fists clenched at his sides, nails digging into his palms. "What the fuck…?"

The candles—knocked over, some still flickered , struggling against the cold wind. Flowers—scattered. Liquor bottles, once upright, now lay on their sides, emptied out onto the pavement.

But the worst part?

The tire marks. Thick, black streaks ran up the sidewalk, stopping right at the heart of the memorial—then peeling out, burning rubber over everything.

The site hadn't just been stomped out or kicked over. They *ran it down.*

J-Rock exhaled , stepping forward. Slow. Careful. Reverent. Taurese followed, gripping Clink's FNO flag with both hands, his chest heaving. The fabric was soiled, having been dragged through the dirt by the wind, but he clutched it tight—because it was all that was left.

A broken bottle lay among the wreckage, its jagged shards glinting under the streetlights. The bitter stench of spilled malt liquor still lingered in the air—a mocking reminder of past vigils.

J-Rock's fingers hovered over the tire tracks, his voice cracking. "This ain't right."

Taurese's jaw tightened. "It's not the same. It never will be." His voice was thick, shaking. "My boy… somebody gotta pay for this."

The gang came together, heads bowed, standing in a tight, silent circle.

When the moment of silence was over, Kordell lifted his head toward the house sitting just beyond the ruins, atop its lonely hill. His voice was steady, cold. "All operations down." His eyes burned with something fierce. "It's time we get back. You feel me?"

Taurese shook his head. "My G's… tonight feels like a bad dream. I'm done."

Kordell nodded, his voice low. "Rest up, my brother."

But as he turned—as they all turned—something made him freeze.

Tom's house…

The lights were out, but the window—the one looking on to the memorial—stood wide open. In the darkness, just visible through the shadows, stood a silhouette.

Watching.

CHAPTER 23

ECHOES OF THE GHETTO

NOVEMBER 20TH – 3:10 PM

The Porsche awaited me in the lot, its sleek black exterior gleaming. A single press of the fob awakened the beast, the engine already softly humming by the time I entered. The door closed with a firm click. Ahead, the city beckoned.

I turned down the police scanner. Too much noise. Too much distraction. I needed clarity. One button press and music filled the car, the bass dropping in, deep and measured, thumping in my chest.

The city rolled by in flashes. At first, everything looked golden—the Big East bathed in sunlight, buildings catching the light just right. There was movement, energy, a heartbeat. For a second, it felt… alive.

Then, the shift came. Street by street, the brightness dimmed. Smiles faded. The hopeful turned weary. Postures slumped, eyes dulled. The energy changed. The hood had its own rhythm, its own language. You either spoke it, or you didn't belong.

The deeper I went, the heavier the air became. Zoom zombies lined the streets. Slumped figures, skin ashy, eyes vacant, bodies drained. They moved like they were caught in slow motion, ghosts in the place they once called home.

Dreams didn't live long here. Not anymore. I gripped the wheel tighter, turned a corner, crossing into FNO territory.

I lowered the music volume. Outside, I peered at boarded-up windows and graffiti-tagged walls marking invisible borders. I could feel silent figures watching from the shadows.

The Porsche purred to a stop. In the glow of the dashboard, I sat there for a beat, fingers tapping against the wheel, eyes scanning the streets. I adjusted my sunglasses.

Then, with a deep breath, I stepped out. The door clicked shut. For a moment, everything held still. Then, a voice drifted through an open apartment window.

"Theodore, Alondra, sit down. It's homework time…"

"Yes, Mommy."

My eyes shifted in their direction. Inside, a mother gathered her kids. Her voice was firm. Warm.

People always saw the projects for the worst of what they were: crime, gangs, and struggle. But a lot of people never saw this—the ones still trying, fighting, and raising kids to be more.

This was why I did what I did. If even one of these kids could push through the cracks… then maybe the future wasn't lost.

My eyes snapped ahead. Beyond a chain-link fence, under the flickering glow of a dying streetlamp—Kordell. Cigar lit, with his back turned.

I climbed the fence, landing lightly. Ahead, Kordell stood, his back facing me, flanked by two of his group. Other FNO members lingered at the outskirts, restless, on edge. I knew they were grieving. Ready for war.

I spoke first. "You know, you're not supposed to keep your back turned. Easy to sneak up on."

Kordell's body stiffened. His shoulders rolled—a fighter bracing for impact. A murmur passed through the group. Hands twitched toward waistbands. Then, Kordell turned.

His expression was razor-sharp. Eyes colder than I'd ever seen. "Really, Dawson? You're gonna show up here like this? Right now?" He brought a lit cigar to his lips.

I held my ground. "I came to offer my condolences. For your boy Clink. Nobody should have to go out like that."

Kordell's face tightened. Grief and fury. "Yeah? And what do you know about how he went out?"

"It's under investigation. I got my best guys on it."

Kordell snapped, "That's it ?"

J Rock moved next to Kordell to show solidarity

I stepped closer, lowering my voice enough to force the whole crew to lean in. "Something's going on, Kordell. Bigger than Clink. Someone else is pulling the strings."

Murmurs rippled through his boys. Restless. Uneasy.

"Whoever you're dealing with isn't just military—he's special ops. Trained. Precise. And he's probably not working alone."

Kordell's fists clenched at his sides. "You think I don't know that? You think I don't see what's happening?"

I took a step forward. "Do you?" My voice cut through the air like a razor. "Because if you start making moves without thinking, you'll lose more than Clink. This ain't just about FNO anymore. This is about control— Someone's playing both sides, and you're walking right into it."

Kordell looked away, jaw tight, chest rising and falling too fast.

We stood there for a long second, staring each other down. I turned to leave, then heard.

"You better handle it. Or the streets will."

I caught the shift in posture. Unity. I scanned both their faces. I replied, "Well, the next body's on you."

That's when one of the younger ones couldn't help himself.

"Man, why should we trust anything you say? Every time I see you, it's on the news—with a badge. So far as I'm concerned, you still a cop."

Kordell muttered—"Taurese—"

Too late.

I grabbed the kid by the collar, slammed him into the wall like Lawrence Taylor on a blindside sack.

I growled, "Listen, I'm not your teacher. I'm your last warning."

Everything stopped.

I heard a couple of windows slam shut in the projects. His boys backed up

Silence dropped like a brick.

But I wasn't here to win them over. I was here to prove a point.

I finally had their attention.

I looked at Kordell. Then at J-Rock. "Keep your head on a swivel."

I adjusted my butter-soft coat.

Turned.

Hopped the fence.

Door shut.

Gone.

Kordell stood still, puffing his cigar. Eyes on me.

Didn't say a word.

Everyone else?

Went back to business.

CHAPTER 24

CLASH OF THE CODES

NOVEMBER 28TH – 8:39 PM

The bounce of the basketball echoed off the empty pavement in the late evening's stillness. Kordell dribbled, his movements slow and almost absent-minded. The game had been a distraction—a temporary escape from the weight pressing against his chest.

But his feet carried him down familiar streets, and they knew where he was going. The memorial had been cleaned up since the last time he saw it, the destruction erased, but the scars still lingered—fewer candles than before, only an ominous glow. The scattered photos had been replaced. None of it could bring Clink back, though.

Kordell came to a slow stop, gripping the ball under his arm as he stared down at the shrine. It had been too long. He exhaled, shaking his head. "Damn, Clink."

The words came out heavier than he expected. He swallowed hard, rolling his shoulders back like it might shake off the tension coiled inside of him. "I just… I couldn't remember you like that, man. That shit had me messed up. I know we're supposed to visit you every day, but…" He dragged a hand over his face, letting out a dry chuckle. "You got me out here talkin' to ghosts."

The wind shifted, the leaves stirring at his feet. He let his gaze drift upward, searching the sky.

And then, the clouds moved. Not in the slow, gradual way they usually did—they split. Wide enough for a sliver of light to peek through, casting a glow over the memorial.

Kordell's breath caught in his throat. "Yo…" His fingers tightened around the ball, and his heartbeat suddenly became loud in his ears.

"Is that you?"

8:52 PM

Lucas sat by the window, fingers twitching against his knee. His eyes flicked to the locked door, then back out the armored window, and the world just beyond his reach.

"How loud do you think a gunshot is?" Tom asked suddenly, eyes still locked on the blade he was sharpening.

Lucas blinked. "I don't know."

"Two-thirty-seven," Tom said. "Guess how loud a bow and arrow is."

Lucas hesitated. "Twenty?"

Tom snorted. "Correct, Junior. One-thirty-five. Right down the middle," he said sarcastically, dragging the blade across the whetstone in one smooth stroke. "Stealth. Learned that from training. The jungle's only rule? Don't get caught."

He was running out of time.

His gaze shifted to the back of the kitchen, landing on Tom. The old man was seated at the table, meticulously sharpening one of his knives. His expression was unreadable. The blade scraped against the whetstone, the rhythmic motion almost hypnotic.

Lucas knew, even if he could get past the locked door, he wouldn't make it far if he made a run for it now. Tom was strong. Trained. Paranoid.

But Lucas was smart too. He took a slow breath and decided.

Across Tom's cluttered kitchen workshop were piles and piles of tech—pieces of drones, exposed circuits, and welding tools. Tom Caldwell, sharp-eyed and steady-handed, had switched to soldering something with intense focus.

Lucas glanced at the door. His mind raced, mapping out every possible route of escape. "I gotta use the bathroom," he said.

Tom didn't look up from his work. "You mean the head. Call it anything else, and you're using a bucket. Understand?"

"Fine."

Tom smirked, holding up a soldered drone wing. "Look at this beauty, kid. Chaos wrapped in precision. You know how much damage I can do with this?"

Lucas forced a nod, his eyes darting to a window across the room. He had noticed earlier that Tom operated his traps with a clicker device, which was set to deactivate parts of the house momentarily as a safeguard. He thought he had figured out the pattern.

As Tom became engrossed in his work again, Lucas moved toward the window. Every step felt like thunder in his ears. But just as he reached out—

Tom moved like lightning.

"Where do you think you're going, kid?"Before Lucas could react, Tom shoved him out of the way of a spring-loaded bear trap. A flash of steel, a sharp cry of pain—two of Tom's fingers fell to the floor. Blood spattered across the table.

Tom screamed, clutching his maimed hand, and he dropped the clicker device. His face changed, eyes glazed over like he was suddenly somewhere else—in another world, another time. His body twisted as if avoiding invisible bullets, knocking pots and pans to the floor. His voice rose in guttural screams, half war cry, half agony.

Lucas backed away, trembling. Tom turned to the stove, igniting the flame and waiting for the coils to turn hot enough to cauterize his mangled hand and stop it from bleeding out.

This was Lucas's chance—the booby trap on the second floor was still disabled. He stumbled out of the kitchen to the living room, making his way down the stairs, his eyes wild with fear and desperation. He yelled bloody murder, banging on the front door, praying that someone—anyone—was listening.

Tom stumbled, hand trembling, and flicked the stove on high. The coils ticked, then hissed behind him.

Then—everything changed.

The pager buzzed louder, then silence. A new kind of silence.

The air shifted. Trees. Smog. Jungle. Insurgents slithered through the swamp, dragging along the wet moss and thick, humid air—air so damp it clung to your throat. Arrows sliced past his ears. Bullets cracked from the tree line. He wasn't in his kitchen anymore. He was back in the swamp. His platoon scattered across the wet earth like ghosts.

His bow lay in the muck.

But how could he draw it?

Two fingers—gone. Here and there. Just…gone.

To the left, his boy walked away again. That sight cracked something—something war never managed to touch. He couldn't let it happen again. No. Not like this.

The pager flared: FRONT—ENTRY—BREACH.

Then—he snapped back.

All of a sudden, he was in the kitchen again. The stove glowed red, and beneath it, the blood that had fallen earlier had begun to bubble—thick and alive—forming boiling, illuminated scabs across the coils. The smell hit next. Iron and burn.

He looked at his hand. Then the coils.

Two fingers gone

He gritted his teeth, stepped forward, and plunged his hand into the fire—

And a warrior's cry echoed through the house.

It was so raw, so full of pain and fury, that even Lucas froze at the front door—his fists still mid-pound.

… and then silence.

8:53 PM

Kordell froze. He pulled his gaze away from the angelic beam of light playing over Clink's memorial and turned toward a sound—a faint banging noise echoing from the direction of Tom's house, followed by muffled screams. *A kid's.* His instincts flared.

"Thanks, Clink."

Kordell's feet were moving before his brain could process. He ran across the road, up the driveway, and bolted up the steps, taking them two at a time.

"Kid! Hold on, I'm coming."

Zzzzzzt. The cold metal of the doorknob sent a violent surge of electricity through Kordell's body. His muscles clenched, his teeth gritted, and the shock threw him backward like a ragdoll. He tumbled down the porch steps, landing hard at the base. His head struck the cracked concrete with a sickening thud.

For a moment, everything was hazy—the world spun, and his ears rang with static. Blood trickled down the back of his head, steaming in the chill of the night air.

But then—clarity.

Adrenaline surged through his veins. His eyes snapped open. Kordell pulled out his phone, his bloody fingers fumbling across the screen. Upstairs, he could hear Tom yelling, "*C'mon, c'mon…*"

Kordell tried to kick his way into the house, but it was as hard as steel. Then, not a second later, without any further battering, a mechanical click sounded, and the front door swung open all by itself.

Still reeling from being zapped, Kordell launched into the foyer, where he was met with the unmistakable smell of sizzling flesh. He covered his mouth with his hoodie sleeve and made his way through to the rear of the abode. He checked his phone again. "Taurese… pick up, man. *Pick up!*"

Kordell crept through the house, clutching the handle of the worn knife he always carried. He could hear movement upstairs and down—muffled steps and shouts, and a faint buzzing sound emanating from somewhere…

9:04 PM

Across town in Newhallville, Taurese stood in the middle of an alley, exchanging bags with jittery customers under a spotty streetlight. His phone buzzed in his pocket.

"Yo, what's good, Kordell?"

"*I caught him, Taurese. I caught him! Tommy's got a kid, man. He's got a kid!*" The urgency in Kordell's voice struck Taurese like a slap.

"What? You sure?"

"*Yes, bro! I'm at the house. He's here. He's here right now!*"

Without another word, Taurese pocketed the product; his customers shouted after him, but he didn't care. He threw his leg over his bike and pedaled furiously, his breath fogging in the cold night air as he raced five miles westward.

Upstairs, Lucas treaded the floorboards carefully. Blood from Tom's mutilated fingers was splattered across his T-shirt. His eyes locked on a small device on Tom's workbench—the claymore clicker. His heart raced.

"This might shut everything down," he whispered to himself. He snatched the clicker and pressed, trying to match a sequence of buttons he had seen Tom use earlier. A faint click echoed through the house. Then, somewhere below, mechanical locks disengaged.

He sensed the basement door unlock, a bolt sliding open with a metallic groan.

Lucas turned, his hand trembling as he gripped the device. He started toward the basement stairs.

"Oliver… please be down there," he whispered.

But before he could descend, a strange man slipped into the corridor.

"*Hey, kid!*" the man hissed.

Lucas froze.

"Kid, you good?" The man looked down at Lucas's bloodied shirt with concern. "Where's Tom?"

Lucas finally found his courage. "H-he's hurt."

The man nodded. "You gotta get outta here. Front door's open, make for that."

"B-but I can't leave yet—my friend might be in the basement!" Lucas's voice trembled with exhaustion and fear.

The man nodded again, his jaw set. "Alright, you go get your friend. I'm gonna handle Tom. I've had enough of this dude…"

Lucas gave a thumbs-up in the dark and disappeared down the basement stairwell.

Kordell inhaled deeply and started up the stairs toward the second floor. His boots creaked against the worn wooden steps. The knife—an old army surplus thing—felt heavy in his hand, slick with sweat.

The buzzing—which he now recognized as Tom's pager—grew louder with every step he took.

At the top of the staircase, Kordell paused, his heartbeat thundering in his ears.

Then, he saw him.

Tom Caldwell stood at the end of the hallway, his face illuminated by a single flickering light bulb overhead. The pager went on shrieking at his belt. His left hand hovered near his belt, missing fingers gushing blood onto the floor. In his right hand, he held a soldering iron, glowing hot as coals in a fire.

His eyes met Kordell's, cold and calculating. "You finally made it, Kordell." Tom's voice was calm, his head tilting.

Kordell gripped his knife, his knuckles turning white. "You're done, Tommy. You're done messing with kids, messing with families. With us. This ends tonight."

Tom smirked, his lips curling into something between amusement and menace.

"You think you're the first to come up here with revenge in your heart, Kordell? You won't be the last."

Kordell took one step forward. Tom's eyes narrowed.

In a flash, Tom hurled the soldering iron straight at Kordell's face.

Kordell dodged, lunging forward, and the two men collided, slamming into the walls, fists swinging.

"FOR CLINK!" Kordell roared, confidence surging with each hook that landed.

Step by fumbling step, Tom retreated from Kordell's blows. Internally, Tom laughed—the guy wasn't hard to lead. All righteous fury, his world painted red. Too easy.

"You're gonna pay for everything, Tommy!" Kordell barked, spit flying from his mouth as he advanced.

Tom's smirk widened into a predator's grin. "Come on then. Show me what you got."

Kordell surged forward again. *Jab, jab, hook. Jab, jab, hook. Cross. Double cross.* He swung with every ounce of strength in his body, but Tom calculated quicker—ducking, weaving, countering.

Then, he grabbed Kordell's wrist mid-swing, twisting it. The sound of bone snapping filled the hallway, and Kordell's face contorted in agony.

Before he could react, Tom yanked him forward by the broken arm and spun him around in one fluid motion.

The window behind him shattered as Kordell's body crashed through the glass. Time seemed to slow as Kordell's silhouette hung in the air, shards of glass sparkling around him like frozen stars.

He hit the ground below with a brutal, final thud.

The incessant buzzing of the pager returned to the forefront. Tom Caldwell's cold eyes flicked downward, scanning the glowing device clipped to his belt, as lines of text flashed: *Multiple insurgents detected.*

Code Red alert.

Locations ground level pinged.

Another intruder. Tom stood by the shattered window, gazing down at Kordell's broken body.

A muscle in his jaw twitched. It wasn't regret, no. But something.

He turned toward the kitchen. One step, then another. Deliberate. Calculated. His hand reached for his weapon of choice—the bow and arrow, oiled and gleaming.

Outside, in the fractured moonlight, he could hear Taurese yelling, "Kordell... Kordell..."

Lucas crept deeper into the basement. The air was damp and heavy, and there was a smell of rust and stale water. A faint flicker of fluorescent light buzzed overhead, casting uneven shadows across the cold concrete walls.

In the corner, inside a huge makeshift metal cage, sat Oliver— pale, eyes wide, but still breathing. The space within was set up like a twisted dormitory: a mini fridge, a cot, and a stack of old comic books.

"*Oliver!*" Lucas whispered as he approached.

Oliver squinted through the thin bars. "...Lucas? Yo, what happened to you, man?"

Lucas smiled. "You should see the other guy. But what happened to you? Have you been down here all this time?"

"Too long, man..." Oliver's eyes glazed over with horrified recollection. "The dude upstairs—he's out of his mind. Keeps talking about war zones and booby traps. Saying these numbers over and over..."

Lucas blinked. "Numbers?"

"Yeah, man. Crazy shit," said Oliver. "Seventy-something, thirty-seven... We gotta get out of here."

Lucas nodded, his mind racing. He examined the cage door, his fingers running over the rusted metal hinges and the thick padlock.

"There's gotta be a way to open this thing," Lucas muttered, yanking the lock as hard as he could.

Oliver glanced toward the ceiling as faint thuds and distant shouts echoed from above.

"Lucas... faster, man. He's coming."

Taurese gazed down in horror at his friend's shattered body on the ground.

Kordell's head lolled to the side. His breathing was shallow. His eyes, unfocused, fluttered open for a brief second.

"My legs, man… my legs…"

Taurese knelt on the patchy grass. "I'mma get you out of here."

Kordell's hand gripped his sleeve, shaking, desperate. "Don't… let him… win…" Then, his eyes widened. "Watch out!"

Taurese's head snapped up—

It was Tom. Hanging out the second-floor window, bow raised. The floodlight from inside framed him in shadows, turning him into something less than a man, something more like a predator.

The bowstring stretched, and the arrow locked onto them.

Taurese jerked his gun up, finger tight on the trigger. But he couldn't fire—not while dragging Kordell.

He had to move.

Fast.

Tom leaned to the right, trying to angle the shot. The window frame creaked under his weight.

Just then, his balance tipped—his fingers flexing to catch himself before he tumbled forward into the yard.

The bowstring loosened. The shot was lost.

Tom snarled and ducked back inside the house. His pager vibrated, and his eyes flicked to the alert: House alarms disengaged.

He cursed.

The boy.

9:31 PM

Outside, Taurese hauled Kordell's useless body deeper into the backyard, past Tom's father's rusted truck.

Kordell's breaths were sharp, pain evident in every exhale. He grabbed at Taurese's arm, pulling weakly. "Yo… leave me."

Taurese ignored him, kept moving.

"Forget about me. Get him."

Taurese's grip tightened. "No. I ain't leaving you."

And then—

The world exploded.

A screeching blast of sound shattered the night, hundreds of decibels of pure chaos.

Music. Louder than should be humanly possible. The ground shook beneath them. Taurese's head whipped toward the house.

The back porch door burst open, and Tom stepped out.

His left hand was mangled, two fingers missing. Blood streaked his forearm, but his grip on the bow was unwavering.

There were three arrows clenched between his teeth.

Tom ripped his blood-soaked shirt down the middle, tossing the pieces aside, revealing beneath an ancient tattoo: an inked warrior, bow raised, arrows flying in multiple directions.

Tom's eyes gleamed in the moonlight, primal, unshaken. "Two against one," he laughed. "I know this dance."

Taurese dropped Kordell and stepped backward, his grip tightening around his 9mm pistol. Even with the chaos blaring around them from unseen speakers, Tom moved like an animal—silent, precise. He held the bow aloft with what was left of his left hand and pulled the string taut with his right. "Hoo-rah…" he mouthed.

"DOWN!" Taurese shouted, diving sideways onto Kordell's body.

The arrow tore through the night air, embedding itself into the dirt where he'd just been standing. Tom nocked another arrow.

Taurese whipped around and trained his pistol on Tom's head.

"You only got six shots in that thing, Taurese."

"More than enough," he spat back.

Neither man moved. Kordell, lying broken on the ground, watched as two forces of nature stared each other down.

Then—Tom's arrow launched, the exact moment Taurese squeezed the trigger.

The arrow whistled through the air, slicing the space between the two men by a hair. It embedded itself deep into the rear tire of the rusted truck with a deafening pop.

Both men scrambled—Kordell dragged himself behind the truck's rear wheel, and Taurese dove sideways, sliding behind a rusted barbecue grill that clattered as it toppled over.

Kordell gasped for air, his face pressed against gravel. His body was failing, but his will wasn't. He gritted his teeth, using only his upper body to pull himself further behind the truck.

From behind the grill, Taurese popped up and fired three quick shots. *BANG! BANG! BANG!*

But Tom was ready. He ducked, then leapt back onto the porch where there was cover. He looked almost bored, as if the firefight was just another day at the office. "Wasting bullets, Taurese…"

Taurese cursed under his breath. His fingers shook as he ejected the clip to see what was left. "Just one," he whispered to himself. He kissed the final round, slid the clip back in, and chambered the round. "Make it count."

He took aim at the porch, spotting Tom's head peeking out from behind a wooden pillar. Then, he pulled the trigger.

Click. The gun jammed. "*No, no, no, no…*" he stammered.

Tom crept out from behind his cover and grinned wide. He advanced quickly, drawing another arrow from his quiver, and aimed at Taurese's heart.

He let it fly.

The faint whistle of the projectile was the last sound Taurese heard before it struck him squarely in the shoulder.

Then—*BOOM!*

An explosion of wood and metal. J-Rock's car tore through the backyard, slamming into the porch pillar and sending splinters and debris flying. The impact rattled the whole structure.

Tom stumbled backward, nearly losing his footing. His eyes snapped to Taurese, still upright somehow.

He took aim again.

BAM!

The car skidded into the second pillar. Half the porch collapsed, and Tom jumped out of the path of the falling roof only just in time.

The passenger door flew open in Taurese's face.

"GET IN!" J-Rock shouted.

Taurese started heaving Kordell into the backseat, his struck shoulder muscle throbbing. He was just tucking Kordell's crippled legs inside when Tom jumped out from nowhere, ready to shoot.

J-Rock threw the car in reverse, hoping to take out the last pillar—the one that would collapse the entire porch.

He missed. The car lurched and smashed into the side of the building instead.

"Damn it!" J-Rock growled, slamming the gear shift.

Kordell was still hanging on, fingers white-knuckled on the seat.

Taurese yanked him the rest of the way in, breath tight. "I can't have you losing your legs, man—I ain't wheeling your ass around in no chair."

THUNK. An arrow punched straight through the roof.

J-Rock jerked the wheel, tires screaming as the car peeled away from the house, scraping against the siding.

Just then, *sirens*.

As soon as J-Rock launched onto the street outside Tom's house, the first squad car came barreling down right behind them.

J-Rock blew the stop sign. The car tore through the intersection, engine roaring.

10:22 PM

A second squad car slowed outside the mangled home.

Tom stepped forward, hand dripping blood, body tense. His chance to end this—gone. He turned as the cop stepped out of the vehicle.

"Sir, you alright?"

Tom wiped the blood from his eyes, shaking his head. "Don't worry about me. My attackers. Go get *them*." He pointed his non-ruined hand at J-Rock's car, speeding away in the distance.

The cop hesitated—then jumped back in the squad car, engine roaring as it sped off to join the chase.

Still battling with the padlock on Oliver's cage, Lucas heard tires screeching outside, the echoes of gunfire rattling in his ears. Then, police sirens.

"Go, go, go!" screamed Oliver.

Lucas nodded. He leapt into action, sailing up the basement stairs, through the kitchen, and to the front door. But the moment his fingers grazed the door handle—

Click.

A thunderous sound as every lock in the house re-engaged. The mechanical whir of unseen gears shifting, securing the basement. Smoked security glass descended over the windows.

Lucas's stomach lurched. He spun backward, heart slamming against his ribs as Tom's amplified voice boomed through the house.

"Get to the table. Now."

Lucas hesitated.

"NOW, JUNIOR."

His legs moved before his mind could catch up, stumbling backward toward the staircase. His hand shot out to the nearest window. Locked. Metal plating had secured itself over the glass. He tested another—same result.

The house was no longer just a house.

Now *it* was a cage again.

His breath came out in short, panicked bursts as he forced himself up the stairs. One step. Then another. The hallway stretched out longer than before, the familiar walls now foreign.

He yanked open a bedroom door, then gasped.

Tom stood in the doorway, looking like hell. His face was swollen; one eye was nearly shut from a brutal punch. His lower lip was cracked, with dried blood at the edges. His knuckles were raw, bruised, torn open.

But Lucas's stomach churned when his gaze dropped to Tom's left hand—the pinky and ring fingers blasted clean off. One of the stumps was still crudely wrapped in a makeshift bandage, the visible skin around both burned and blackened. The stench of seared flesh lingered on him, mixed with sweat and gunpowder.

Lucas swallowed hard.

Tom stepped closer. His breathing was ragged, but his voice was low and measured. "Three tours." He flexed his injured hand, then slammed it onto the table. "I went through three tours. Lost friends. Lost sleep. But I kept my goddamn limbs."

His nostrils flared, chest rising and falling with sharp, contained rage.

"Then *you* come back into my life." He shoved his mangled hand toward Lucas. "And in less than a week—THIS happens."

Lucas felt his throat tighten. Tom's glare pinned him to the wall behind.

"You see this?" Tom growled, leaning in. "LOOK AT IT."

Lucas's eyes burned, but he didn't blink. He couldn't. His hands clenched into fists in his lap, his shoulders rigid. He had never seen Tom like this.

It was worse than anger, whatever was in his eyes. Worse than disappointment.

Betrayal?

Tom leaned back, inhaling through his nose before exhaling through his teeth. His gaze flickered over Lucas's tear-streaked face—stone cold. Finally, he stepped back, reaching into his pocket.

He pressed the clicker. Lucas realized with a jolt that he had dropped it in his scramble to find Oliver.

The sound of bolts and reinforced panels sliding into place echoed through the walls. The device in Tom's hand blinked red.

Lucas knew: Every exit had been sealed, every trap armed.

Tom exhaled, eyes boring deep into Lucas's.

"You're grounded."

CHAPTER 25

THE WARRANT WHISPERER

NOVEMBER 30TH – 1:38 PM

The courthouse doors loomed ahead like a damn mausoleum. Old, stiff, and full of relics, who thought *they* held the keys to justice. I walked in without hesitation, my dress shoes tapping against the marble floors. I wasn't here to play politics, I wasn't here to kiss rings—I was here to get a warrant.

And I wasn't leaving without it.

The scent of old wood and stale authority hung in the air as I pushed through to Judge Helmsley's office. His chambers were cluttered with dusty law books and outdated decor, a time capsule of a man who refused to evolve.

I didn't knock. Didn't pause. I walked in, removed my sunglasses, and folded them before setting them on his desk.

Helmsley barely looked up from his paperwork. "What can I do for you, Detective?"

I leaned in, my voice low, firm. "I need that warrant we discussed earlier."

Helmsley exhaled, as if I was wasting his precious time. "For what?"

"Thomas Caldwell. We have reason to believe he's behind the recent kidnappings."

He raised an eyebrow. "You have a suspicion."

I reached into my coat, pulled out a manila envelope, and slid it across his desk. Helmsley opened it: surveillance photos of Caldwell's house. Angles of the yard, the porch, the driveway—and the *BEWARE OF LANDMINES* sign nailed to the front porch gate.

Helmsley sighed long and slow, closing the file with disappointment. "We can't do anything with this."

I leaned further forward. "What do you mean you can't do anything with this? We've got missing kids out here."

Helmsley folded his hands, his expression blank. "Caldwell is a highly decorated veteran. I won't let you tarnish his name without substantial evidence."

I slapped my palm against his desk. "He's got 'Beware of Landmines' all over his property! What kind of civilian does that?"

Helmsley leaned back, unfazed. "Halloween decorations. He put them up in October and never took them down. We've had multiple complaints, but guess what? That's his property. There's no crime in that."

I stared at him, disgusted. "This man is dangerous. We pulled his military records. He's got a history of trip mines, booby traps, *and landmines*. That's his specialty. That's what he does."

Helmsley shrugged. "Doesn't prove a thing. A man's past doesn't convict his present. If you want a warrant, bring me *real* evidence."

I let out a sharp, bitter laugh, shaking my head. "We've known each other for how long? And this is how you do me?"

Helmsley met my stare. "Yeah, but guess what? I'm the judge, and you're the detective. That means I tell you what parameters you stay within." He scoffed. "You are never above the law, Dawson. And you sure as hell don't want to be below it."

I clenched my jaw so tight I thought I might crack a molar.

"Hey, Alex—"

His expression darkened instantly. His back went straight, his shoulders tensed. "The robe is on," he said coldly.

I chuckled bitterly. "You've been outshined by those millennial judges, and it's soured your soul."

Helmsley's jaw ticked.

I pressed on. "All you care about is campaigning for your next political agenda. Playing it safe. You don't make decisions—you avoid them. Every time this city needed you, you dropped the ball."

Helmsley leaned forward, his voice lowering into something venomous. "You know what, Dawson?" He folded his hands, smirking. "You remind me of a dog that runs to the door every time someone rings the bell."

Then, he leaned in further, our faces inches apart.

"But you know what? The door is never for the dog."

And then, right there in my face—

"ROOF!"

I flinched, more out of confusion than anything. "Screw you, Alex." I pointed in his face. "You're failing this city, hang the robe up."

Helmsley snapped his fingers. "Bailiff. Get this animal out of my chambers."

The door behind me swung open, and two officers marched in.

I let out a breath of dry amusement. "You actually called the cops?"

And then one of them had the nerve to put their hands on me. I damn near dislocated his arm out of its socket.

"Get the hell off me!"

They stumbled back, but they grabbed me again, and this time didn't let go. My dress shoes slipped against the polished floor, my body twisting as they dragged me toward the door.

Helmsley's voice followed me out. "The door is *never* for the dog, Dawson."

Five minutes later, I was thrown unceremoniously out of the courthouse. In the chill afternoon air, I adjusted my coat, straightened my shirt, and pulled out my phone.

"James. Bad news. Warrant's been denied. We're go have to do something else."

2:47 PM

The city rolled past in a blur of steel and pavement as I drove. Hunter and I sat in the unmarked patrol car in silence. We were en route to another case when the radio crackled to life.

"Dawson, we got eyes on Jake."

I grabbed the receiver. "Go."

Cash's voice came through, steady. *"First time he's been to school all month. He was flirting with some girl, then grabbed his basketball and started walking. He's headed toward the East Side courts."*

I exhaled, gripping the wheel. "Be right over. Do not let him out of your sight."

"Copy that."

Hunter started flipping through the case file. The drive to the basketball court felt longer than it should have, and by the time we pulled up, late afternoon shadows were stretching across the asphalt. The smell of fried batter from distant food trucks wafted in through the driver-side window.

And there he was, basketball in hand, walking onto the court like nothing in the world was wrong. I killed the engine.

Hunter lifted the printed street cam photo, holding it up against the windshield. The reflection in the glass lined up with the kid on the court.

She nodded. "That's him."

I pushed open the door, stepping onto the pavement. Jake's sneakers scuffed against the concrete as he shot hoops, solo. Swish, into the net.

I whistled. "Mind if I get in on this?"

The ball stopped mid-bounce. Jake turned, brows raised. "Oh, hell nah. Old heads wanna hoop?"

I tilted my head. "Scared?"

He spun the ball on his fingers, letting it roll to his palm before tossing it over. "Show me somethin' then."

I caught the ball clean, lined up my shot—then bulldozed my way into the paint.

Jake held his ground, but I was bigger, stronger. One step. Two. Then, I spun off him, sank the shot, and let the ball bounce away.

Game.

Jake bent over, hands on his knees, sucking in air. "Man… y'all cheated."

I clapped him on the back. "Fair's fair."

Hunter finally stepped forward. "Jake. We need to check your phone."

His smirk faded, eyes flicking toward the bench, toward his bag. Then, just like that, he bolted.

I didn't move. Neither did Hunter. She just spoke.

"We're here about Lucas and Oliver. They're in trouble."

Jake froze mid-step. Then, slowly, he turned back.

I pulled him in by the shoulder. "We already matched up the street cam footage. We know you were there. What we need to know is, what happened?"

Jake swallowed, his voice quieter now. "We were just messing around. Ding-dong ditching. That's it."

The words slammed into me like a gut punch.

I took a step closer. "What street?"

Jake gulped. "29th Big East Hill Section, near Old Mill Street."

Hunter and I locked eyes. My phone was in my hand before it even registered that I was dialing James.

"Sure thing," he replied. "Pulling footage from the centralized cameras now. Give me a couple of hours."

"One hour," I pressed. "Time's ticking."

Hunter grabbed her coat. "Let's move."

Jake shifted on the court, rubbing his hands against his jeans like he could wipe away his guilt.

I watched him carefully. "You should've come to us sooner." I kept my voice low, understanding. "Instead, you skipped school. Didn't go home. Didn't tell a soul."

Jake pawed the asphalt with the toe of his shoe.

"And when we checked your place, you know what we found?"

His breath hitched.

I leaned in slightly. "A pair of jeans stained with eggs."

Jake swallowed. "That don't mean nothin'."

I arched a brow. "No?"

He forced a smirk. "I could've been cooking breakfast."

I smiled. "You weren't cooking shit."

Jake laughed nervously. "I'm sorry. Really. I know I should've told someone. I just didn't wanna get in trouble."

My patience was gone. "Your friends could be in real danger."

Hunter stepped in. "Dawson, he's just a kid."

"So what?" I shot back. "Actions have repercussions. You want soft? Soft gets people killed."

Hunter shook her head. "Fear doesn't build trust, Dawson."

Jake shifted uncomfortably. "Y'all fight like my parents."

I smirked, but there was no warmth in it. "Cute." I turned to leave. "Stay near your phone, Jake. Don't make me send the boys after you."

He let out a shaky laugh. "Yeah, yeah…"

Once we were back in the car, Hunter gave me a sideways glance. "You're impossible."

CHAPTER 26

THE SILENT SETUP

She had spent years escaping his shadow. Now, she could move on. Really, she already had.

Samantha Caldwell—no, Samantha Teller now. A new name. A new life. A new beginning. No more detectives, no more military.

The justice of the peace ceremony was small. Low profile. No big church. No grand spectacle. Just two people stepping forward together. Her new husband, Daniel Teller, slid her engagement ring off her left hand, and on went a diamond wedding band.

A fresh start.

But somewhere in the back of her mind, Tom's voice had still echoed: "*You will never wear a ring again.*" She'd shaken it off then.

Days passed. Cards, gifts, and congratulations poured in. Packages lay stacked by the door, some from friends, some from family. A lot of gifts from the in-laws. She opened them one by one, her husband beside her in his armchair. A blender. Martini glasses. A cloth napkin set.

Then came the last one, a medium-sized box. It was heavy. She shook it. *Solid.*

A thrill ran through her. *Something expensive*? She glanced at Daniel. "We got another one." She turned the box over in her hands—and that's when she noticed it.

The wrapping paper.

The texture felt off.

Then she saw… a *handprint*. Red. Pressed into the paper.

Her stomach turned, but she laughed it off. "Creepy." She ripped the wrapping off without another thought.

The moment she lifted the box—

BOOM.

An explosion shattered the room. Glass, wood, and fire tore through the air, spinning her world upside down.

Her ears rang. Her vision blurred. Her body crashed against the floor.

She heard screams. Her husband's voice—distant, distorted.

Smoke filled the air. Samantha coughed, she tried to move—but she couldn't.

Again, Tom's voice whispered in her mind. *"You will never wear a ring again…"*

When Samantha woke, she wasn't at home. Through hazy vision, she saw white walls, white ceilings. Machinery bleeped beside her bed, playing out the dissonant music of her vital signs.

Daniel sat beside her in a plastic chair. He smiled when he found her gaze, but something in his eyes had changed.

Samantha tried to rise to a sitting position, but her hand ached. She looked down—her ring finger was missing, a stub bandaged over.

"He was right." Her voice came out as a croak.

Some part of her felt, in the hours that passed afterward, that she was sitting in a wreckage of her own making. *Tommy's disappearance…* She'd blamed Tom for everything. It had turned him cold when he needed warmth. And she had filled her own void with someone else's arms.

"Sorry," she whispered into the pillow. Daniel, asleep in the chair beside her, didn't rouse.

CHAPTER 27

DETOURS AND DEVIATIONS

NOVEMBER 30TH – 4:32 PM

Johnston switched on the television in the precinct and tuned to the correct channel.

"Reporting live—we're on the scene of a shocking explosion that has left one woman critically injured. Authorities have confirmed that the victim is one Samantha Teller, formerly Caldwell—a name many will remember from years ago, in connection to a tragic, unattended drowning incident involving her son. Now, in a twist of fate, Samantha finds herself fighting for her own life.

"According to initial reports, a mysterious package was delivered to her residence just moments before the blast. The explosion tore through the home, leaving widespread destruction and triggering a full-scale investigation.

"She was rushed to the hospital, where doctors remain tight-lipped about her condition. But sources indicate that she suffered severe injuries and may be facing a long road to recovery.

"Authorities are now working to determine whether this was a targeted attack or a tragic coincidence. Stay with us for updates as this story develops.

"This is Amy Reddins, reporting live for On-Scene Media, Channel 8."

I turned off the television. Around me, the detectives stood motionless, eyes locked on the black screen.

Tonight was a turning point.

"We should've gotten to her sooner," I said, wiping a hand down my beard.

Sandra walked up and leaned on my shoulder.

I grimaced. "Dump that boyfriend of yours yet?"

She rolled her eyes, lips tugging into the hint of a smirk. "Don't start."

Hunter let out a tepid chuckle. I turned to face the team.

"All right, listen up. Hunter and I are going to confront Tom. Johnston, Cash—you're heading straight to the hospital." I sighed. "She's under strict security due to the nature of the attack. No games. No detours. I want her interviewed."

Johnston exchanged a glance with Cash, who gave a short nod. "Understood."

I turned to Sandra, reaching into my coat and tossing her a radio. "Take this. You're not from this precinct, but if anything goes sideways, which it shouldn't, I want you on comms."

Sandra caught it with ease, clipping it to her belt.

I addressed the team again. "If anything goes down, you radio me." I pulled on my coat and made for the door.

"Let's move."

5:40 PM

The headlights of Johnston and Cash's unmarked police vehicle cut through the thick mist as they pulled up to the Big East Hospital. Detective Cash stepped out of the car, stretching his broad shoulders. His jacket hung loose over his frame, but his expression was sharp.

"Alright. You hang back and keep an eye on anyone coming or going from the building."

Detective Johnston nodded from the driver's seat. "Go get 'em."

The lobby was sterile and cold, the hum of fluorescent lights casting pale shadows on the linoleum floors. Cash approached the reception desk, flashing his badge and warrant.

"Detective Clayton Cash, Big East Police. I need to speak to Samantha Teller. Now."

The nurse flagged down the attending doctor, a middle-aged man with a thin mustache and tired eyes.

"Detective, she's in no condition to talk," he explained. "The explosion may have left her traumatized. I can't authorize this."

Cash's face tightened, and his voice dropped an octave.

"Listen to me real close, Doc. There's a kid out there—probably scared, probably hurt. Every second we waste here, that kid gets further away. And that woman in there may know something relevant.

"Now, I'm holding a warrant. Either you let me in that room, or I'll have you locked up for obstruction of justice faster than you can stutter out another excuse."

The doctor swallowed hard and stepped aside. "Fine…"

The nurse handed over the list of room assignments. Cash gave the doctor one last hard stare before stepping through the double doors into the patient wing.

In a room at the end of the hall, guarded by a couple of rent-a-cops, Tom's ex-wife sat in a wheelchair, her frail body shrouded in a thin hospital blanket. Her face bore fresh scars, and her eyes, sunken and glassy, darted toward the window before settling on Cash.

"Hi there," Cash said softly, stepping into the room. "I'm Detective Cash. I think you've met my boss before—Detective Dawson."

She blinked slowly, her lips trembling. "Every time you people show up… something bad happens."

Cash knelt in front of her chair, his voice gentle but firm. "I know you've been through hell, ma'am. But I need your help. There's a kid out there—a kid who doesn't deserve any of this. We know about your ex-husband's history. We need to know if you can help us find this kid."

Her hands, weak and trembling, moved over her lap. Her voice was barely above a whisper.

"The woods… It's in the woods. He buried—no, he hid something. I tried… I tried to stop him…"

Cash leaned in closer, his brows furrowed. "Where? Where in the woods? What did he hide?"

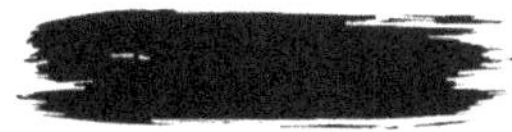

5:11 PM

The sleek black car tore down the empty streets, headlights cutting through the fog. I gripped the wheel tightly, knuckles white, as the tires screeched around corners. Hunter held onto the sealed envelope in her lap, glancing at it every few moments.

We passed an alleyway where I could see a mugging was about to take place—a figure lurking behind a couple of folks in the shadows.

Hunter leaned forward. "Dawson! Someone's going to get grabbed!"

My eyes flicked to the rearview mirror, jaw tightening. "We don't have time for that. Call it in. Let the other uniforms handle it."

Hunter hesitated. "But—"

"Let them handle it."

Hunter nodded, grabbing the radio. "This is Detective Hunter. Possible mugging, corner of 5th and Grover. Uniforms needed on-site. *ASAP,*" she added, throwing me a look.

I ignored her and kept driving. "Tom thinks he's untouchable. He thinks he's smarter than us. But today, we're flipping the board on him."

Hunter tightened her grip on the sealed envelope, her eyes sharp. "Let's end this."

5:58 PM

The sterile lights above flickered as Detective Clayton Cash leaned closer to Samantha, delicately grasping her limp wrist, wrapped in gauze.

"Listen to me, Samantha," Cash said, his voice low but intense. "I need answers. Now. You don't get to play victim. Like it or not, you are part of this."

Her head snapped up, sunken eyes locking onto his.

"You don't know what I went through!" Samantha hissed, her voice sharp despite its weakness. "You don't know what it was like to be his wife, to live under his roof... Far from here, in another life, in another country, I did what I had to do."

Cash leaned closer, unfazed. "You know what, Samantha? I might not know what you went through, but I know that if you don't start talking, you'll have to live with whatever happens to those kids for the rest of your life. That's blood on your hands."

Samantha froze, her lip trembling. Tears welled in her tired eyes. "You'll never understand! You'll never stop him!"

Then, she shoved Cash aside with surprising force, knocking over a tray of hospital food. In a blink, she was out of the room, the door swinging behind her.

"Hey! Stop her!" Cash barked as he burst into the hallway after her.

Samantha barely made it three feet before the rent-a-cops were on her. She wilted in their grasp, dangling pathetically on the linoleum floor.

"Let her go," Cash yelled, waving off the guards.

Samantha's face was pressed to the cold floor, her voice muffled but frantic. "He's going to kill us all…"

Cash crouched beside her, gripping her shoulder. "Samantha, look at me. Focus!" Then Cash saw it—the numbers tattooed faintly on her wrist, just above the gauze: 78°W.

Cash froze. His mind raced. Suddenly, an image swam to the forefront of his mind, of the knife in the evidence file, the coordinates scratched into the hilt… *37 N.*

Was this a marker for the second half of the coordinates? One longitude, the other latitude?

"What is this? These numbers—what do they mean?"

Samantha's voice dropped to a whisper. "That's… that's where he buried our son, where this all started. Where it ends." Then her eyes went blank.

6:14 PM

Outside, Detective Omar Johnston sat reclined in the passenger seat of the unmarked car, feet propped up on the dashboard. The faint thump of hip-hop played from the speakers as he bobbed his head to the beat.

The radio crackled.

"Johnston! I got something. Meeting you at the car, now!"

Johnston's head snapped up, the relaxed facade dropping instantly. He threw his feet down, silenced the radio, and jumped out of the car just as Cash burst through the hospital doors.

Cash waved a slip of paper in the air. "We got something, man. *Coordinates.* North 37, West 78. We got to talk to Dawson."

Johnston froze for a moment, his expression darkening. "Talk to Dawson? Nah, MAN. We ain't calling Dawson."

Cash frowned. "What? Johnston, this is not a solo act. We're a team. Dawson's going to want to know—"

Johnston shook his head. "We're detectives, right? So, let's go detect." Cash still looked unconvinced. "Plus," Johnston added, "now's the perfect time to swoop in and get the evidence we need, while Dawson's got Tom distracted."

Cash sighed, his shoulders dropping. "Alright. Let's go."

Johnston grinned, plugging the coordinates into his scanner. "Buckle up, partner. We're heading into the woods."

THE AMBUSH ALGORITHM

NOVEMBER 30TH – 6:25 PM

The black Porsche rolled to a slow stop in front of Tom Caldwell's residence, a weathered two-story house with cracked paint, which now I could see was the least of its problems. The muddy front yard was torn up by tire tracks, and I could just spot the dangling back porch roof, which had been ripped to shreds.

Hunter and I stepped out of the vehicle. We walked up the stairs

"You feel that?" Hunter asked softly.

"Yeah," I said, voice low. "Something ain't right."

We approached the steps leading up to the front porch. When my boot hit the bottom step, it shifted under my weight.

I paused, nudging the step with my foot again. It creaked, revealing hinges along the edge, barely visible, but there.

I whistled. "That's shoddy carpentry if ever I saw it."

Hunter knelt, squinting at the hinges, her hand drifting to the holstered gun at her hip. She pushed on the wooden boards, but they wouldn't give. "Locked?"

We continued up the steps. Hunter raised her hand to knock on the door, but before her knuckles met wood, the door creaked open on its own.

Standing there in the entryway was Tom Caldwell, dressed in a worn black shirt, a hunting bow slung across his back. His eyes were hollow, and the faint glow from inside the house cast sharp shadows across his cheekbones.

"Evening, Detectives," Tom said.

I barreled inside. "Where were you last Thursday night, Tom?"

"Nowhere," he said flatly.

Hunter's eyes flicked downward to Tom's left hand, where two fingers were freshly severed, wrapped messily in gauze. "What happened to your hand?" she asked.

Tom's face didn't flinch. "Shaving."

We stood there in silence. Then, Hunter erupted in an anger I hadn't seen before.

"You expect us to believe that?" she screamed. "How about we ask Cage, who ironically is, as we speak, in a cage?"

Tom made to close the door. "I'm not dealing with rookie games tonight. Come back with a warrant, or don't come back at all."

Before it could close fully, Hunter's boot shot forward to jam the door.

From that thin space between the door and the frame, Tom's eyes glinted red. For a moment, his cold mask slipped. "You shouldn't have done that."

Hunter nearly growled at him in response, but I stepped in. "Tom, take your PTSD out on me, not the lady, listen here you might've roamed overseas like a roaring lion... but over here in the Big East, I'm top dog." I slapped my chest

Tom's lip curled. "You think you're ready for what's coming, Dawson? You think you know the rules of this game?" His voice had dropped to a whisper.

I didn't blink. "I don't care about your rules, Tom. I'm here to end your game."

For a long moment, no one moved. Then—

A series of beeps sounded from the region of Tom's waist. He casually unclipped the pager and held it up.

Hunter squinted. "A pager? Seriously?"

Tom grinned maniacally, the screen illuminating his face. Quickly, he pulled a strange device out of his pocket and pressed a single button.

Deep in the woods, closing in on the convergence of those two coordinates, Detectives Omar Johnston, Clayton Cash, and Officer Sandra Dawson moved in quiet formation. The dim beams of their flashlights cut through the fog, revealing twisted tree branches and uneven ground littered with damp leaves.

"Thanks for bringing me along," said Sandra.

Cash nodded. "Figured we might need some backup."

"It shouldn't be much further," said Johnston, his voice strained.

Sandra peered down at the GPS device in her hand. "It's right over here, I'm sure of it. The coordinates match."

Cash stopped walking and squinted. His flashlight caught a glint of metal embedded in the ground thirty feet ahead. "Hold up," he muttered, adjusting his rifle strap.

They listened in the eerie silence. Somewhere, an owl hooted, but beyond that, there was nothing. No wind. No movement. Just the sound of their own breathing and boots crinkling the forest undergrowth.

"We're right on top of it," Sandra said, lowering the GPS and gazing around.

Cash rubbed his chin. "I don't see nothing."

But then—he did. A few feet away, barely visible in the twilight, an infrared beam stretched across the path.

Red. Thin as a hair.

Cash watched as Johnston started to walk on, impatient. "Stop!" he gasped.

Johnston halted, then followed Cash's gaze downward to the beam. "Oh, shit. Good catch." He stepped backward, away from the sensor.

A faint *click* sounded beneath his boot.

Johnson's face paled. "Oh, shit."

Twenty feet ahead, a stone slab shifted off what had looked up till then like a large rock, revealing a hidden mechanism.

Sandra squinted into its depths. "Is that…a grave?"

A sharp whining sound, like metal scraping metal, filled the air. Hydraulic pistons hissed to life. Up out of the chasm, displacing a bed of moss and matted leaves, rose a massive firearm, which locked onto the three of them.

Beep. Beep. Beep.

Johnston's breath hitched.

"Oh, sh—"

The Gatling gun spun to life.

In a flash, multiple arrows with shining metal tips launched in their direction. In one swift motion, Johnston lunged forward, shoving Sandra behind a nearby tree. Her head hit the ground hard where a knotted tree root was jutting, and she lay there, unconscious.

Johnston winced at a pain in his abdomen. He looked down. An arrow was stuck smack in between two of his ribs. He found a second buried deep into his shoulder. Blood spurted from his wounds as he staggered backward, gasping for air.

But Johnston wasn't done. With trembling hands, he raised his service pistol and fired a single, desperate shot at the turret. Cash darted to the right, towards him.

BANG.

Simultaneously, another arrow pierced his throat.

His shot had hit its mark, though, striking the rotary mechanism of the Gatling gun and causing the turret to jerk sharply to the right, throwing off its trajectory.

Unable to smirk—hell, unable to breathe—Johnston fell to his knees. His eyes drifted over to Sandra, facedown on the forest floor. Then, to Cash, whom he realized had taken two of the three arrows in the second volley—the ones intended for him.

The first had struck Cash's back, piercing his lung. The second embedded itself in his side, narrowly missing his heart.

Both men crumpled to the ground.

The scent of blood and burning metal washed over them. The malfunctioning Gatling gun continued to whir and buzz above them.

Supine, Detective Cash reached for the radio clipped to his vest. He gritted his teeth, fighting against the searing pain in his chest as he pulled it up to his mouth.

"Mayday... Mayday..." His voice was barely a rasp. "This is Detective Clayton Cash. Officer down. Repeat, officer down. Johnston hit... multiple wounds... Sandra Dawson is unconscious, Mayday, Mayday..."

The radio crackled.

Static.

"What the hell was that?" I took a step closer to Tom in the doorway, my voice a growl. Hunter's radio crackled faintly on her hip.

"Mayday... Mayday..."

I froze. I grabbed the radio and held it to my face. "Cash? What's going on?" No response: the signal on our end didn't seem to be going through. Then, Cash's voice again.

"Mayday... Johnston hit... Sandra down... Mayday..."

The blood drained from Hunter's face. "Sandra?"

Panic welled in my chest. I could feel my heart beating madly, thundering right up against the metal plate at my sternum like a war drum.

"You better run back to your team, Dawson," Tom said coolly.

I didn't even attempt a retort—I was already halfway to the Porsche. Hunter jumped into the passenger seat beside me, and we were off.

Tom watched the black Porsche speed away with mild amusement. "Well, that was fun." He raised the clicker to eye level.

Click. Click.

The pager blinked red—switching from *TARGET ENGAGE* to *RETRIEVE*.

With a long press of the button, a mechanical whirr echoed overhead. From the third-floor attic, the chimney split open, and a high-speed drone emerged—hovering into the sky with surgical precision. A millisecond later, it flew off toward the pre-programmed location.

Tom glanced at his military watch and adjusted it to fifteen minutes sharp—his personal window of operations.

Time to clean up.

The engine roared as the Porsche accelerated recklessly down the narrow residential streets.

"Signal Four!" I barked, voice frantic. "We need the 29s. We need them en route to Johnston and Cash's location, now!"

Hunter's fingers flew across the radio controls. "Dispatch, this is Detective Hunter. We need immediate police backup—Sector 29. Does anyone have their coordinates? Officers down. Repeat, officers down!"

The dispatcher's voice crackled to life. *"Hunter, we hear you. We have their coordinates, got 'em when they picked up Sandra, texting to you now. But Sector 29 is stretched thin. We'll divert nearby units."*

I slammed my fist against the steering wheel and grabbed the receiver from Hunter. "Every available unit—DO IT NOW."

The dispatcher hesitated before replying. *"Roger that. Units are being diverted. ETA… fifteen minutes."*

"That's too long…"

Cash lay on the ground, consciousness fading in and out. His fingers twitched. His breathing was shallow. His back and chest burned where the two arrows were embedded deep; each inhalation was a battle itself.

"Johnston…" His voice rasped, "Stay with me, man… just stay with me…"

Then, a whirring noise sounded from above.

———

He tried to look up, but he couldn't move. Couldn't turn his head.

But he knew that sound.

A drone.

Another attack? Screaming in pain, Cash managed to lift his neck up an inch.

The whirring grew louder, closing in like a vulture… but the drone didn't strike.

Instead, there came a heavy metallic *clang* as it hooked onto the Gatling gun. With a hydraulic hiss, it airlifted the heavy firearm away, disappearing into the sky.

"Jesus…"

Then—footsteps. Heavy boots.

Coming back to finish us off? Cash thought wildly, feeling his senses leave him.

He wasn't going to make it. His breath hitched, shallow, fading…

A voice.

"We got him!"

A rush of movement. A dark silhouette loomed over him—not a reaper, not an executioner—but a firefighter, kneeling. A gurney being walked up behind him.

"Stay with me, buddy. You're going to be alright…"

Lights, red and white, flashed across his eyes.

Then- darkness.

CHAPTER 29

LIFELINES

NOVEMBER 30TH – 7:21 PM

Τhe Porsche weaved in and out of traffic, narrowly missing side mirrors and pedestrians crossing intersections. My foot was glued to the gas pedal as I downshifted, the engine growling like an angry animal. Horns blared in protest as the Porsche bolted through a red light without hesitation.

Hunter, clutching the dashboard, looked at me. "Dawson, I thought you knew how to drive!"

I kept my eyes on the road ahead. "You want me to slow down, Hunter? Or do you want me to get there before they're dead?"

Hunter said nothing. Maybe she didn't get it—that for me, every turn of the wheel, every gear shift, every heartbeat felt like an eternity. The thought of my niece lying injured—or worse—lit a fire in my chest.

Hunter's voice broke in. "Dawson, we'll get there in time. Johnston and Cash—they're fighters. And Sandra, she's tough."

I nodded, my jaw set. The radio crackled again.

"This is Sector 29—we have officers on the scene."

Hunter leaned back in her seat, exhaling. "Hold on, Sandra… hold on, Johnston… we're coming."

7:22 PM

"We're moving them out!" the lead medic ordered.

The team began their grueling hike out of the dense woods, carrying the wounded detectives on gurneys. IV bags dangled from poles, and heart monitors beeped rhythmically as life-support measures were administered on the move.

An RV with off-road capabilities waited at the clearing, its lights cutting through the fog. At the perimeter of the woods, dozens of emergency vehicles had gathered—ambulances, fire trucks, and police cruisers. Flashing lights bathed the forest in blue and red hues.

Cash's eyes fluttered, his chest rising and falling with each strained breath.

Sandra remained limp on her stretcher, a thin line of blood streaking her cheek, mascara staining the pouches below her eyes.

The Porsche skidded into the clearing, its tires carving deep grooves into the dirt. The engine growled one last time before I slammed the vehicle into park. Before the dust settled, Hunter and I were already out of the car, sprinting toward the gurneys.

"Johnston! Cash! Sandra!" I yelled through the chaos. We rushed to Sandra's stretcher. Hunter gripped her hand, brushing hair away from her pale face. "Sandra? Can you hear me?" Hunter looked up at me, eyes brimming. "She's breathing."

I let out the breath I'd been holding for who knows how long. *Alive.* I turned to crouch beside Johnston. "Hold on, Omar. Stay with us. We've got you."

On the next gurney, Cash's eyes pulled open, and he coughed weakly. "Dawson… it was a trap… don't… trust…"

His eyes fluttered closed.

I barked at one of the paramedics, "They need to be moved—now." Then, I turned to Hunter. "And we need to figure out what the hell just happened."

As we watched our brothers and sisters in arms get loaded onto ambulances, Hunter grabbed my shoulder. "We're not giving up. Do you hear me?" She closed her eyes against the tears staining her face. "As long as they're still breathing, we've got hope…"

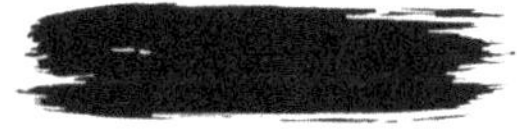

9:55 PM

At the hospital, I could only imagine what was going on behind closed doors. Cash's body, convulsing under the paramedic's hands? Johnston's throat torn open by that arrow, his chest barely rising as doctors strapped a brace around him, preparing for surgery? All I'd seen was all that blood painting their gurneys—too much blood.

And Sandra… thankfully, in not as critical condition. But still, harmed.

I felt like I was in a bad dream. I blinked, and a moment later, Barbara was right in my face. Her red-rimmed eyes were filled with something I'd never seen in her before—pure, boiling rage. She shoved a finger into my chest.

"You better find out who did this to Cash and Johnston," she spat. "And you better put them in the ground."

I stared at her. She wasn't crying. She wasn't breaking down.

She was threatening *me*.

Barbara—the woman who'd spent decades laughing at me from behind that precinct desk, answering calls, filing reports, taking coffee orders. She turned on her heel and stormed out of the ER.

I stood there, panting, the smells of blood and antiseptic filling my nostrils.

Hunter was talking. Someone else was talking. None of it reached me.

All I knew was that I needed to get out of there.

I needed to *handle* this.

CHAPTER 30

THE CONFRONTATION

The drive to the precinct was a blur. My mind was still in that ER, replaying Johnston's chest struggling to rise, Cash's fingers twitching as they hauled him onto the table. I barely noticed when I screeched into the lot, the Porsche jerking to a stop in front of the entrance.

I left the door open, the engine running.

One of the late-night detectives, a young guy barely out of the academy, glanced up from his cigarette.

"Hey, you left your car on."

I shot him a look. "Congratulations, you just got promoted to valet."

I stormed into the doors of the precinct and punched the elevator button. On the way up to the 10th floor, I paced like a man condemned, heart pounding. I felt my defib teetering on the impulse to activate.

But I couldn't calm myself. Every time I blinked, I saw the paramedics working on Johnston. The blood. The oxygen mask over Cash's face…

The doors slid open. I stepped out.

In the middle of the night, the precinct was dead silent except for the faint crackle of radios and the buzz of overhead lights. I walked past the rows of empty desks, past the bullpen.

Barbara's words still rang in my ears: *You better find out who did this.* My boots thudded against the linoleum.

Chief Avery's door was cracked open. I could see him inside, hunched over his desk, listening to the radio, sweat glistening under the desk lamp.

Perhaps he knew I was coming.

He just didn't know how bad it was about to get.

I kicked the door open. Avery barely flinched.

"Dawson…" He exhaled slowly. "I know."

I stepped forward, voice low, tight, dangerous. "No, Avery— you *knew.*"

His face didn't move, but his massive form straightened up in his chair.

"You knew this was too much for them," I sputtered. "I told you this job was too dangerous for rookies. I *told* you. But you didn't listen. And now they're hanging on by a thread."

Avery leaned back again in his chair. "This is the job, Dawson." His voice was firm but tired. "This is what we signed up for."

I let out a bitter laugh. "Yeah?" I stepped closer, shaking my head. "But you're not out there, are you? You're not in the dirt, dodging arrows, dragging kids out of the mud."

His jaw clenched—dangerous.

I went on. "You sit in this office. You sit here while they bleed out in the field." I looked at the framed photo of his wife on his desk.

Without breaking eye contact, I grabbed the photo and slammed it down.

CRASH.

Glass flew all over the place. Avery shot up from his chair.

"Watch your mouth, Dawson."

But I wasn't finished. I grabbed his gold-plated nameplate off the desk, ripped it from its stand, and shoved it into his chest.

"You don't deserve this office. You don't deserve this nameplate. You don't deserve to sit here while my team bleeds out in the woods."

Avery's nostrils flared. "You better back down, Detective."

I stepped right into his face.

"Make me."

He swung first.

I ducked. Drove my shoulder straight into his ribs.

The desk exploded under us, papers flying, coffee spilling everywhere.

Avery was strong. Stronger even than I expected. He wrapped his arms around me, lifted me clean off my feet, and slammed me onto the desk.

Pain shot through my back. I rolled off fast and caught him with a right hook. His jaw snapped to the side, but he barely staggered.

Damn. What a effing tank.

He charged, slamming me into the filing cabinet. The metal drawers rattled and upended.

I gasped, the air knocked out of me. Finally, his fist came down—and caught my ribs.

White-hot pain exploded behind my eyes. The defibrillator seared into my skin, threatening to activate, to quell the racing of my unequipped heart…

But I just didn't care anymore. I went for Avery's Leadership Award, grabbed it off the wall, and went to smash it over his giant head—

"ENOUGH!" he bellowed, arm raised in the air in defense of my impending blow. He held his other palm to his forehead, where a stream of blood was trickling down onto the carpet.

We stood there, the two of us, panting.

Then his voice dropped, hoarse, raw. "You want revenge? You want justice?" He clenched his fist. "Go find who did this. End it, Dawson. Before anyone else dies."

I nodded, wiped the blood from my own mouth.

"Come at me again, and you're fucking suspended."

I nodded again. "Thanks, Chief."

Then I turned, stepped over the wreckage of his office, and walked out.

The door slammed behind me.

CHAPTER 31

THE CALCULATED DISTRACTION

NOVEMBER 30TH – 6:56 PM

Tom moved swiftly up the stairs, knocking twice on the bedroom door.

"Hey, Junior, change of plans. The company had to leave early."

A pause.

"Go ahead and eat—Pops has business to handle tonight. You understand?"

A voice murmured from inside. "R-roger that."

Tom smirked. "Good. That's my boy."

As soon as he descended into the kitchen, his entire demeanor shifted to tactician. He tapped a preset command on the pager. Then, he stepped onto the front porch, rolling his shoulders.

The sky was illuminated red and blue—not from the police, but from his drone, returning right on schedule.

The mission was complete.

The drone descended from 3,000 feet. With his remote control, he guided it back into its dock in the chimney hatch manually, bringing it down smooth as a precision airstrike. He pulled the Gatling gun from its grappling hook. It was weighty and warm from use in his arms. With practiced ease, he ejected the ammo drum and removed the black box—a recording module.

He held the black box up to the moonlight. Like a piece of treasure.

"Oh, it's *on* tonight." He pressed *RETRIEVE* once more.

The drone slid back inside the chimney hatch. With a soft hiss, the panel sealed.

Next stop: the War Room. Tom entered the dimly lit bunker, pulling an MRE from the shelf. He ripped it open, took a bite— then grimaced.

"Ugh. The nasty kind." Shrugging, he sat down, booting up a terminal.

The screen illuminated in eerie blue, replaying the 'battle' in the woods. He switched it over to the projector, which painted the bunker walls like bruises with the incompetence of Dawson's rookies—arrows launching, screams slicing, the girl knocked out like a paper doll, Johnston's heavy body crumpling to the ground.

Tom watched. Analyzed. His smirk grew wider as he rewound certain delicious moments.

Blue light flickers from the projector, painting the bunker walls like bruises.

Footage plays. Arrows slicing. Screams. Johnston drops.

"Oh, there you go, Johnston… thought you had a shot," Tom mutters.

He doesn't turn—but he knows.

"When you're hunting… everything has a scent. Sweat. Fear. Guilt. You don't need eyes or ears when the air tells you everything."

Tom keeps his eyes forward.

"That's jungle recon 101. You pick up on presence before a shadow even lands. So, when you crept in here, yeah… I knew.

You know, Junior… I've done tours. Elite units. No sleep deep in the swamps. But these last weeks? Right here, trying to protect you?"

He lifts his hand—showing two fingers missing.

"I lost these because you didn't listen. I said Don't touch the perimeter. You touched it. I said Don't trigger the failsafes. You set 'em off like it was a joke.

You have a practice of disobeying orders. And I've followed every single one I was ever given. My whole life. Did everything my government told me to do. Played the part. Wore the patch. Buried the friends.

And this… this is what buys you freedom?"

He scoffs, low.

"But you called the head the bathroom. That tells me everything I need to know. You're not built for this.

And all I asked for was five minutes. Just! Five damn minutes to watch this in peace."

He hits pause. Johnston's body freezes mid-fall on screen. Then he presses play again.

Tom chews. Swallows. Rewinds. "Play it again."Lucas's eyes redden. His jaw tightens. The breath in his chest coils. His stomach knots.

"They came after my son."Lucas flinched."Dawson. Johnston. All of them. They thought they could take what's mine."

Lucas swallows hard. A tear breaks loose. Silence. Lucas steps forward, barely audible. "If you hurt the cops to protect your son… then who am I?"

Tom doesn't answer at first. He keeps his gaze on the flickering screen. Then slowly turns his head—just enough ."You're the reason I don't sleep."

The footage continues.

Onscreen: the chaos resumes.

Behind him, Lucas stands broken, silent, drenched in blue.

CHAPTER 32

BREAKING POINT

DECEMBER 1ST — 5:15 PM

Parking under the bridge, under a sky thick with gloom, the Porsche's headlights reflected off the rain-slick pavement, casting fractured light across the crime scene tape. The weight of the ambush—and of the fight with Avery—still lingered in my throat. Hunter and I exited the car and moved toward James, working on this new case. The forensic specialist glanced up, exhaustion etched into his brow.

I knelt. "Working hard, or hardly working?"

"Man, I've been here all day," James muttered, rubbing his temples. "You guys don't need to be out here, though." He looked up at Hunter. "Not after what happened. You should be resting."

I scoffed. "Resting? When the people who did this are still breathing? Not a chance."

James exhaled, shifting gears. "Someone called from the hospital. Apparently, Cash remembers an aerial device at the scene." He sighed. "I checked the drone database, but nothing came up. It's like it doesn't exist."

Hunter said, "It couldn't have been him. He was right in front of us when it happened."

I snapped, "Yeah? Then we need to figure out how the hell his hands stay clean while the rest of us bleed."

Hunter pressed, "We've got to go visit Aspen at the military base directly—find out what his technological capabilities really are."

I cut her off short. "Detective mode is off."

I stepped forward, voice like gravel. "I'm paying him a visit, Face-to-face."

I looked them, dead in their eyes. "And if you find out he had anything to do with that ambush… don't tell me. "Because that's the difference between me walking him out in cuffs—or him not walking out at all." Hunter tensed.

James shook his head. "Dawson, listen to me. If you're going after him, you better bring an army. This guy is dangerous. *Lethal.*"

I stood. "No, James. I'm the dangerous one." The words carried a finality that even James couldn't counter. He and Hunter exchanged a wary glance. Dawson's coming apart, it seemed to communicate.

I turned toward the crime scene, gripping the yellow tape. "Clean this up! My hands began to tremble. My face was slicked with sweat. I clutched my chest.

James noticed first. "Dawson, you okay?" I waved him off.

Hunter sprung into action. "Dawson, sit down."

"I'm *fine*," I snapped, doubling over as another wave of pain hit.

"Medic!" Hunter called out. "Get a medic to the scene, now!"

"No," I gritted out, stumbling backward. "I'm not going to lie in a hospital bed next to Cash and Johnston…"

But my body betrayed me. My knees buckled, and I barely caught myself on the hood of a parked car. While my heart faltered in real time, the world blurred. Inside my chest, an electrical misfire, a system on the brink of collapse…

Then, I closed my eyes and breathed—one, two—and my heart slowed.

Good enough.

"I'm not going," I snarled, shoving past the medics.

Hunter slammed the car door and rushed toward me. "Dawson—"

But I was already walking, heading straight down the street, right into the glare of the city's surveillance cameras.

James shook his head. "This mission's going to kill him before the enemy does."

5:39 PM

Back at the forensics lab, James waved Hunter and me over to his computer monitor. "You've got to see this."

Hunter asked, "What's that?"

James typed rapidly, pulling up further surveillance footage—the one I had specifically asked him to check after someone defaced Clink's memorial. My stomach tightened.

James glanced up at me. "Guess who destroyed the memorial?" He tapped the keyboard again, fast-forwarding the footage.

The screen flickered, the feed jumping ahead. A truck rumbled into view, its headlights cutting through the darkness like twin beacons. It rolled to a slow stop near the makeshift memorial—candles, flowers, and photos left behind by grieving families. Then, a sharp clang as the driver's side door slammed shut.

Tom Caldwell stood motionless in front of the memorial, his expression unreadable. Then, he climbed back into the truck.

The engine roared to life.

And he hit the gas.

The truck surged forward, plowing through the memorial with ruthless force. Flowers crumpled under the weight of steel. Pictures were torn from their moorings, sent flying like dead leaves in the wind.

I rounded on Hunter. I couldn't believe what I was seeing.

Her hands balled into fists. James's fingers drummed against the desk, eyes locked onto the footage. I could feel my pulse thundering in my ears.

This wasn't just a case anymore.

This was a war.

And time was running out.

6:03 PM

Twenty minutes later, James came back to me with the best news I'd ever heard.

"You just might get your warrant, Charlie." He indicated his computer screen. "I dug up more footage. The absolute *lynchpin*."

A smug look of satisfaction crossed James's face. "I searched to see if there were any doorbell cameras on the streets where those kids might've been on Mischief Night." He tapped the screen. "Here's the footage."

James tapped the keyboard. "Cameras A through D—four-house radius." The screen lit up.

Three silhouettes appeared—grainy, slow-moving, hoodies up, cartons of eggs in hand.

"That's them," James said. "Jake, Oliver, and Lucas." One of the figures peeled off at the edge of the yard.

"Tallest one's Jake," I muttered. "So that means Lucas and Oliver kept moving."

We watched them walk past the house, and then James pointed out. "Right here— Two of them. Up the block ."

The footage played.

"They never come back out," James said. "No retreat. No return. Like they got swallowed."

Hunter leaned forward. "Which house is that?"

James clicked to the next feed. "We've got another cam posted up the street. Six, maybe seven houses past this one."

He played it. Empty street. No figures. No boys.

"They don't show up on that one either. They vanish somewhere in between." Then James turned and looked me dead in the eye. "You know whose house is two doors down in the direction they were heading?"

Beat.

"Thomas T. Caldwell."

I did not speak; I just stared at the screen. At that stretch of quiet suburban dark. I knew that street. Did not say it out loud. No need to. It wasn't ironclad proof. But it lined up like crosshairs.

James said quietly, "We can submit this to Helmsley.

Hunter added, "If he doesn't think it's enough—"

I cut them both off.

"The last time I submitted evidence to Helmsley, he sent his boys to do what the gavel couldn't."

"If I walk into that courthouse again, without five signed warrants to search those houses..."

I'll be the first to fight a chief and judge in 48 hours."

Silence followed.

It was too late, the wrecking ball had already been set in motion.

I stood there between them all—Hunter, James, and the computer—grinding my teeth into powder. "Fine, then. To hell with warrants. Maybe it's time I just took things into my own hands."

James stopped typing. His fingers hovered over the keyboard, his expression suddenly guarded. "Charlie, listen—"

I cut him off. "No. You listen. Caldwell thinks he runs the goddamn world. Thinks he can declare martial law on sovereign land. We're going to teach him otherwise."

James shook his head. "You're making this personal."

My eyes flashed red. "It's been personal since the moment those kids disappeared." I turned to Hunter. "Go get Helmsley on the line. Maybe you can talk some sense into him."

Hunter nodded, ever my lieutenant. She sped off. I was grateful for the quick obedience; unsure I'd have enough fight left to spare come morning.

James waved in my face. "Dawson, *listen to me*. If you go after him alone, you're gonna die."

"Give me the infrared glasses, James."

James didn't move. "Dawson—"

I turned, voice like steel. "Hand them over."

James swallowed hard and did as he was told. I secured them on my belt, checked my revolver, spun the chamber once—and snapped it shut.

Two extra speed loaders. Strapped in place.

I'm not waiting till morning to get told no on a warrant.

James took a breath. "I'm calling it in."

I froze. Turned my head just slightly. "If you do that… we're done."

For the first time in our friendship, I wasn't bluffing.

James shook his head. "Man, don't do this." He was stalling. Trying to buy time.

I pulled the collar of my shirt down and looked at my chest. The defib charge indicator read: 47%. That's all I had left. Half power. Enough to get it done.

James was still talking, still trying to talk me out of the risk. But my mind wasn't on the defibrillator. He shifted in his chair. "I just don't want you walking into something blind, man."

"No." My tone was final. "I'll handle this my way."

James looked at me long and hard. Then, with a sigh, he nodded. "Just don't walk into any booby traps."

I grinned. "Well, if I do, let's make sure he regrets setting them."

CHAPTER 33

SOMETHING HUMAN

NOVEMBER 30TH – 7:17 PM

The Evening light dimmed and streamed through the cracked blinds, streaking across the dusty floor. Tom sat at the kitchen table, tapping his fork against the edge of his plate. His venison sat untouched, but to him, they were a victory. Last night was a win—a strategic maneuver, a step closer to control. He felt like a war general surveying the battlefield after a decisive strike.

Across from him, Lucas sat stiffly, stirring his cereal with the slow, distracted motions of a boy lost in thought. His eyes flicked between Tom and the tablet screen propped up on the counter—the same screen that had replayed the video all morning.

Tom knew the look. Something was bothering him.

"What's going on, Junior?" Tom asked, his voice casual but firm.

Lucas hesitated, eyes locked on his bowl. "Nothing. Just thinking. I, uh… I was thinking about visiting Oliver."

Tom took another bite, chewing slowly, considering. "Yeah? You miss your buddy?"

Lucas nodded. "Yeah."

"He... will be leaving soon. Don't worry, he'll be safe." Tom narrowed his eyes. "That's all that's on your mind?"

Tom's jaw tightened. Silence ached between them while Tom considered this change in Lucas's demeanor. Then, with the skill of a seasoned tactician, he pivoted.

"Anyhow, the news said both of those cops are still alive, clinging to life. No harm, no foul." Tom grimaced—then, suddenly, he had an idea. He raised his voice into a higher pitch. "Have you ever heard the story about Grandpa?"

Lucas blinked. "Huh?"

Tom leaned forward, resting his elbows on the table. "Tell me about your parents, Junior," he answered himself in his normal tone of voice.

Luca's eyes darted back and forth, caught off guard. "Uh... I don't really—"

"My father was a military man," Tom interrupted, voice slipping into an altogether different tone—deep, distant, as if he was sinking into another time. "He was a warrior. Lived by the gun. Died by the gun..."

Lucas watched as Tom's eyes darkened, his gaze unfocused. If only the boy knew how he'd cracked open a door into Tom's buried past.

"I remember our last hunting trip together..."

The scent of pine needles filled the crisp morning air. A younger Tom, barely in his teens, knelt beside his father in the damp leaves, their boots sinking slightly into the earth. His father's red-and-white flannel shifted as he reached down, handing Tom a bow.

"You take the shot this time, son," his father murmured, stepping off to the side, watching on proudly as only a father could.

Tom's fingers curled around the trigger, pulling it back, heart pounding. A deer padded into the clearing ahead, its ears twitching.

Then, everything unraveled in an instant.

A misstep. A startled movement. The high-power caliber gun snapped Tom forward, twisting his body.

The gunshot rang through the forest.

Then—silence.

His father lay there, unmoving. Blood seeping into the cold earth.

Tom stumbled backward, dropping the still-warm rifle, his breath coming in short gasps.

The rifle lay beside his father like a grief-stricken widow that jumped onto the pyre. The same weapon that had been his father's shield, time and time again. The one that had become his undoing.

Tom stood mutely at the table, lost in another world outside this room, his lips repeating something indecipherable over and over.

For the first time since meeting Tom, Lucas saw something in his eyes—something fractured.

Then Tom seemed to snap out of it. He rubbed his hands together absently. "After that day," he murmured, "I swore I'd never touch a gun again." He traced a line with his left hand, less two fingers. "Bows and arrows are not unpredictable, no misfires, no jamming, and no ricocheting. That's all I use now…"

Lucas watched him carefully. "W-what day?"

Tom's jaw tightened. "I don't trust 'em!" he hurled the words into a void. "Live by the gun. Die by the gun."

The words echoed in the room.

Lucas swallowed. He had expected Tom to be a monster, even a cold-hearted killer. But now he wasn't sure what he was looking at. Something human beneath the war machine? Something fragile?

Tom pushed back from the table, wiping his mouth with the back of his hand. His moment of vulnerability was over.

"You wanted to see Oliver, right?" Tom said, standing up.

Lucas hesitated, then nodded.

Tom gave a small smirk. "Alright."

CHAPTER 34

THE CRASH OUT

DECEMBER 1ST – 12:38 AM

Rain hammered the Porsche's windshield, lightning splitting the sky in violent cracks. The city blurred past in neon streaks, but I wasn't looking.

I checked the battery level again: now at 43%. Dwindling faster than I'd hoped. Not enough for a second chance. Not enough for a mistake.

My hands flexed over the wheel—black leather gloves. Zip ties. Handcuffs. Ammo. Tight. My mind flashed back to the desert—the military fatigues, the beret, the bow and arrows strapped to my back…

This was going to be a bang-out—soldier against soldier. Two men trained for war, racing toward a collision neither could escape.

No scanner, no radio, no backup.

Just me and him. The bastard crossed the line when he went after my detectives. Hell, he crossed the line when he shattered my niece's world.

I knew I wasn't thinking straight—not that I cared. Who in their right mind would be thinking right after something like this?

I wove through traffic, pushing the engine hard, picturing Tom Caldwell's face, grinding to a pulp beneath my boot…

James's voice was grave. "He's going to do it."

"He's going to do what?" Hunter shot back. She had returned from her unproductive phone call with the courthouse to find Dawson had left the precinct without her.

"Tom. Something's about to go down, one way or the other. Dawson's going to need backup," James urged. "He told me not to call anything in."

"And you listened?" Hunter shook her head. "Doesn't matter. I'm on my way."

Tom glanced up at the dark clouds. Rain trickled down upon his face, but it didn't bother him. It felt nice.

"Junior," he called toward the open front door. "Get in your room. It's going to be a bumpy night."

He pressed a button. The door slammed shut. Locked. The windows sealed tight. He gazed out at the quiet street, a predator waiting for the challenge of its equal.

"Oorah," he whispered.

1:01 AM

"All units, Dawson has designated a no-go perimeter. Stay clear."

I cut the engine. For half a breath, I sat in the dark, listening to the rain hammering the roof. Then, I stepped out.

Boots hit the wet pavement. My breath was steady. My hands were loose at my sides. I walked up the driveway like I was walking into hell.

Because I was.

The house loomed ahead, blackened windows, and in them, the eyes of a dead man staring back at me.

I was going to fuck him up. Even if I had to crawl on hands and knees under those trap door porch steps.

No hesitation. No second thoughts.

 I approached the door.

The inside looked like a burial bunker—steel-ribbed, zero give.

I kneaded a lump of C-4 like chewing gum, slapped two blobs onto the hinges.

Kneeled right outside the doorway. Before I could thumb the detonator,

the lock clicked open—

but the top latch held fast.

Fine by me.

I drove my shoulder through the frame.

The door caved like a shotgun blast hit it.

I stepped back—revolver up—muzzle sweeping four corners, illuminated by flickering fluorescent lights in what felt like an eerie barracks.

I cleared corner one—around the bend—

And there he stood.

Thomas T. Caldwell.

Fatigues on, and a glaze over his eyes—to let me know he was ready like hell.

"How are the rookies?"

His voice bounced off raw drywall. I didn't flinch.

1:08 AM

"You set the time, Tom. I'm just here to keep it."

I shoulder-holstered my gun, cracked my knuckles like dry ice—and we—went at it.

He shifted fast into military Krav Maga style—two sharp elbows, a hammer back-fist—followed by close-quarter exchanges: clean, tactical, precise.

I swung and missed, spun around, and came back with a headbutt to get in close quarters so I could lunge for that cursed pager—but it was gone.

He coiled, foot arcing for a flying knee.

SWOOSH—I sidestepped, hit him with an uppercut. He countered—two overhand rights, one jaw, bone on bone.

**This wasn't a fight.

This was war—a savage collision between soldier and cop.

Then—*Zzzzzzt.*** Static.

The same interference from the diner?

But his eyes were telling me it wasn't him—as he blood-lust locked on me alone.

We both swung, hitting each other at the same time.

We staggered back and collided again, each landing a simultaneous hook.

BEEP. BEEP. East wall.

My eyes widened.

"Shit—someone else brought fireworks."

I wrenched him into a pinwheel choke, shoving him toward the breach—

BOOM.

The east wall blew inward—plaster snowed, studs split like wishbones.

The blast hurled us backwards, slamming us into a support column.

My shoulder tore loose. My draw arm dangled, useless.

Ears ringing, I lay propped up by debris.

The crunching of glass started from a distance and got closer—sounds like tactical boots.

A masked figure stepped through the smoke and debris, then knelt—the visor inches from my face.

"No backup, huh?

Guess Mr. Lone Wolf turned this into a suicide mission."

I looked down.

The defibrillator on my chest flashed angry-red like a countdown.

The .357 lay inches from my left fingertips.

Caldwell clawed for his bow, leaving a thin trail of blood behind him.

The figure stepped forward—with a boot STOMP— bending Tom's fingers backwards.

He roared, "Stay away from my son!"

"The kid is to come home. NACA thinks he's clean."

The boot twisted.

"So I'm only going to ask this once—where is he?"

Her voice—so cold and calculated.

 I lay there, tunnel vision narrowed.

Yeah, well… genius with no cavalry.

What else is new?

The rookies have already bled.

This Big East is burning from the inside out.

And the department?

Well…we've buried too many good ones.

even if it takes my blood to keep them standing—

(I inhaled a slow breath)

—It's worth every drop.

The last beep echoed in my head.

A WORD FROM THE CREATORS

I know what you're thinking right now: *Where is this story going?*

Let me start by saying, thank you, to everyone who participated in bringing this book and project to life. This isn't just a book; it's the beginning of something bigger.

And hey, we didn't just write a book—we made a movie, too! So, if you want to experience this story in a whole new way, be sure to check out Ding Dong Ditch™: the movie.

As you can probably tell by where we left our hero, Dawson, raging on a dangerous warpath that could very well kill him—we're far from finished. There's so much more to come in this series and beyond. Your support keeps us going—whether it's a follow on Instagram (@MaxVisionFilms), a simple hashtag #dingdongditchmovie, sharing the film, or leaving a book review. Every little bit helps—but without your support, this world does not grow. Demand the next chapter.

Thank you, and God bless.

MAXVISION TEAM

Contributors and Collaborators on This Project

Written by Noz

Derrick Meade Genece

Raymond James Meade III – Story Development Support

Kayli Johnson – Editor

Monica Cooke – Editor

Chaz Camron – Editor

InkRebel – Illustrator

Alex Prokop – Beta Reader

Amie Melillo – Beta Reader

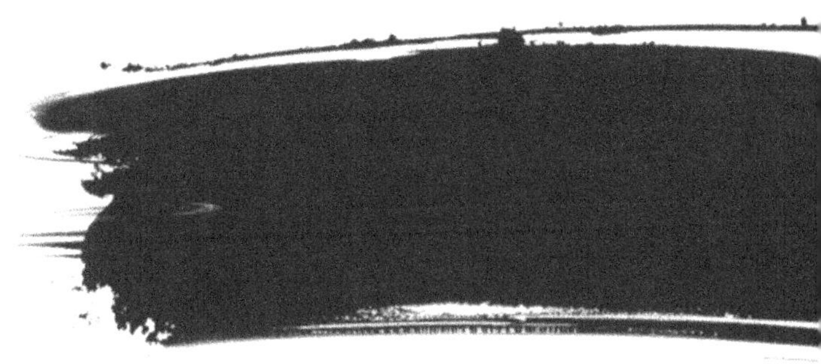

CHARACTER LIST

DETECTIVE CHARLES "CHARLIE" DAWSON

With a long black leather trench coat draped with a revolver crossbody holster, Dawson moves like a relic of another time—one that plays by different rules. He's seen it all, lived through it, and carried the weight of every case that was never due. The world wants him to evolve, soften, and adjust to the times. But Dawson isn't here to adapt—he's here to restore the feeling.

He rolls through the Big East in a sleek black Porsche, flashing lights cutting through the night. His name alone carries weight, and anyone under his command falls in line or gets left behind. But this time, the deck is stacked against him—a new hand of rookies to break in, a new love interest to complicate things, and a city that no longer plays fair. Can he hold his ground, or will this new era finally put Dawson in the crossfire?

THOMAS "TOM" CALDWELL

Tom is one of the ghosts of the Jungle Recon, an operative who was forged in a special forces unit and handpicked by Commander

Aspen. He and Jungle Recon turned the tide of wars with nothing but precision, strategy, and sheer force. A bow and arrow is his weapon of choice. Explosives come second.

Tom doesn't just survive—he thrives on the hunt. He seeks out the strongest leader in any group, whether a gang or the police department, testing their limits and measuring their worth. He needs a challenge to feel alive, always searching for the next opponent who can push him to the edge. Either you're with the creed, or he'll break protocol to enforce it. And if you think you can predict his next move, you're already too late.

LUCAS BENNETT

Mischievous and quick on his feet, Lucas is the kind of kid who turns boredom into adventure. Whether it's sneaking out late or spending his allowance on elaborate pranks like ding dong ditching, he lives for the rush. But one night of mischief is about to change everything.

Lucas becomes the center of a dangerous game he never signed up for. He's sharp, resourceful, and more resilient than most kids his age, but survival instincts can only take him so far. Now trapped in a world he doesn't understand, Lucas will have to figure out if escape is an option—or if he's already part of something bigger than himself.

DR. JAMES LANGSTON

The brains behind the badge, James is The Big East's go-to forensic scientist, hacker, and surveillance expert—all wrapped up in one high-IQ, lab-coat-wearing mastermind. Criminal law? He studied it. CSI? He lives for it. Evidence? He sees what others miss.

James doesn't just pull records and run fingerprints—he builds the state-of-the-art tools that give Dawson and his squad the upper hand. Surveillance rigs, tracking devices, forensic enhancements—whatever it takes to take down the creeps that slip through the cracks. He's the silent force behind every major bust, the unseen weapon in Dawson's arsenal.

DETECTIVE EMILY HUNTER

Thrown into the most cutthroat department in The Big East, Emily Hunter had every reason to take the easy road—but she didn't. Highly decorated and battle-tested, she earned her place the hard way, refusing to let being one of the only women on the squad define her. Now, as a rookie standing shoulder to shoulder with Detective Dawson, she's in the fire, tackling the most twisted cases the Big East Hill Section has ever seen. No shortcuts, no favors—just grit, instinct, and the drive to prove she belongs. The only question left is, how far is she willing to go?

DETECTIVE CLAYTON CASH

Cash is a detective who mostly plays good cop—but when he turns bad cop, no force of evil can withstand his brute strength. Every squad needs an undeniable piece, and Cash brings balance and power to the team. Dawson leans on Cash as his personality pulls the squad deeper into every clue—sometimes too deep for the rookies, sometimes right into the heart of a cold case, exactly where Dawson likes to be. The rare ones know exactly what that means.

DETECTIVE OMAR JOHNSTON

Hot-headed, ambitious, and constantly pushing the limit—Detective Omar Johnston isn't just driven; he's relentless. But is it pure determination or something deeper that keeps him teetering on the edge, throwing himself into harm's way? His best work comes when he feels tested. Sharp and polished, he carries himself with confidence, but his fiery attitude often feels like overcompensation. Straight from patrol to detective, he skipped the usual grind, and he knew eyes were on him. The question is—how far will he go to prove he has what it takes?

KORDELL, J-ROCK, TAURESE, AND "CLINK"

These four form a formidable gang that runs one Section of The Big East like a well-oiled machine. Kordell and his crew get tangled up with notorious Tom Caldwell, but eventually Tom's cruelty becomes too much to bear—even for thugs as hard as these.

KELSEY ROSE

Kelsey is a bombshell of a reporter—both in looks and in terms of the stories she hounds and drops. She's got a soft spot for Detective Dawson, and their eyes meet more than once in our story—whether it's over yellow crime scene tape, or over a bottle of wine.

DANIELLE MARCELLA

Owner and Chief Editor of Real Free Speech, Danielle Marcella runs one of the last independent newspaper mills, a rare survivor in a city where politics have corrupted the press into extinction.

While others folded under pressure, she stood firm, refusing to let the truth die. She believes in Dawson's plan when few others do, making her both an ally and a target. But Real Free Speech isn't just any newspaper mill—there's something different about it, something hidden beneath the headlines. Only those paying close attention will uncover its true role in The Big East.

BRADLEY CAGE

This ex-Jungle Recon operative was exiled for breaking the unit's biggest rule—no gunpowder. Since then, he's lost his way, straying further from his brothers and slipping into the grip of the street drug Zoom. He spends his days hanging with the lowest of the low, a shadow of the soldier he once was. His addiction has dulled his edge, his presence almost pitiful. But don't be fooled—beneath the wreckage of his choices, Cage is still one of the deadliest soldiers out there. His skills haven't left him—they're just waiting for the right moment to resurface.

SAMANTHA TELLER

Tom Caldwell's ex-wife, Samantha, is a kind-hearted woman in her mid-40s who has endured immense suffering, struggling to rebuild her life after losing her son and separating from Tom. Their divorce, fueled by Tom's relentless blaming and abandonment issues, left her emotionally scarred. After returning from a honeymoon cruise with her new husband, an unmarked package at her doorstep explodes, leaving her with severe injuries and driving her to the brink of despair … will she get revenge?

COMMANDER ASPEN

Commander Aspen, the most decorated officer in the region, is a towering figure in military circles—a war hero on paper and a strategist in reality. Many of his most significant victories were sealed by tactics others refused to acknowledge, often the work of Tom Caldwell.

His win-at-all-costs approach delivered results, but at a price. Now, his legacy is a battlefield—a monument built on compromise, shadowed by the moral lines he's crossed. Aspen's presence looms large, his grandeur undeniable, but beneath it all lies a question no medal can answer: Was it worth it?

(other minor characters)

Paxton: James's right-hand man in the lab, another forensics tech at The Big East Precinct

Barbara: Receptionist to the stars at The Big East Precinct

Natalie Dobbs: The precinct's media liaison

Oliver and Jake: Lucas's two best friends

Martha Anderson: Grandmother of Timmy, another kid long missing

Edie Pilot and Dan Thompson: News reporters

Vincent Kane: Dawson's controversial old partner, with whom he shares bad blood

Karl Bronson: Tom's old associate in Jungle Recon (does not appear in this story)

DING DONG
DITCH

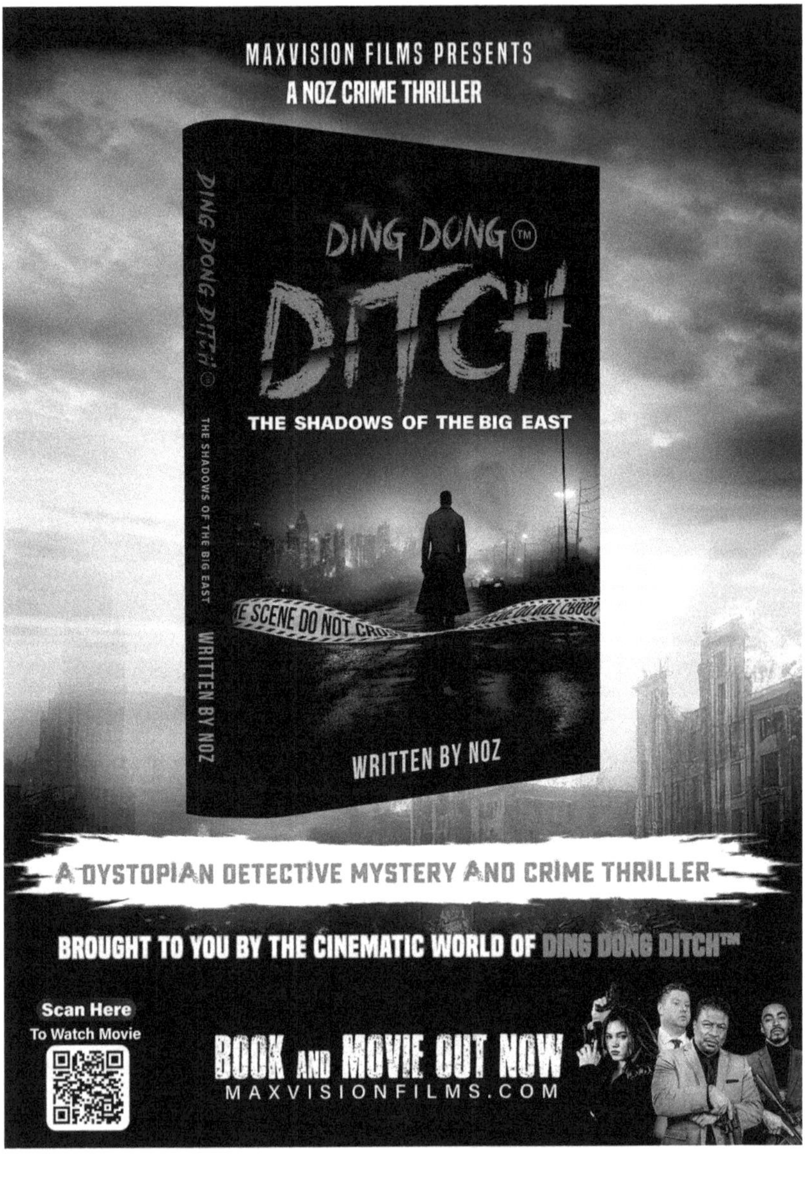
MAXVISION FILMS PRESENTS
A NOZ CRIME THRILLER
DING DONG DITCH
THE SHADOWS OF THE BIG EAST
WRITTEN BY NOZ
A DYSTOPIAN DETECTIVE MYSTERY AND CRIME THRILLER
BROUGHT TO YOU BY THE CINEMATIC WORLD OF DING DONG DITCH™
Scan Here
To Watch Movie
BOOK AND MOVIE OUT NOW
MAXVISIONFILMS.COM

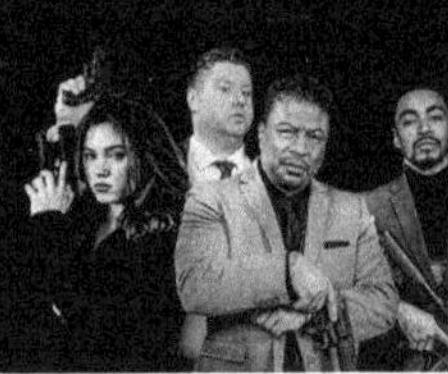

DING DONG
DITCH
EPISODE
OUT N
THE SHADOWS OF THE BIG EAST